TWEEDLEDUMB AND TWEEDLEDIE

WONDERLAND DETECTIVE AGENCY BOOK 3

JEANNIE WYCHERLEY

Tweedledumb and Tweedledie:
Wonderland Detective Agency Book 3
by

JEANNIE WYCHERLEY

Copyright © 2021 Jeannie Wycherley
Bark at the Moon Books
All rights reserved

Sign up for Jeannie's newsletter: https://www.
subscribepage.com/JeannieWycherleyWonky
Tweedledumb and Tweedledie was edited by Christine L Baker
Cover design by Ravenborn Covers
Formatting by Pink Elephant Designs
Proofing by Johnny Bon Bon

Please note: This book is set in England in the United Kingdom. It
uses British English spellings and idioms.

CHAPTER 1

Panting noisily, I clutched the lamp post to steady myself as I hooked a tiny stone out of the back of my running shoe. Dawn was breaking over Peachstone Market. This was a view I could never tire of.

Unlike most of Tumble Town, Peachstone Market was a sizable square open to the elements. This location had to be, as far as I was aware, one of the few places in Tumble Town where you could see an expanse of sky. And Mother Nature had elected to put on a beautiful display this warm July morning. It promised to be a decent enough summer's day. The pastel of the blue would deepen to a gorgeous turquoise, but for now the mauves and oranges of the breaking morning electrified the light, and a thin ribbon of red above the tall tenement buildings bordering the square promised that some shepherds would need warning, but of what was anyone's guess.

Because if there were any sheep in Tumble Town, I

hadn't come across them yet. Thank goodness.

There were plenty of odd-looking, smelly creatures without throwing farmyard animals into the mix.

Taking a moment to breathe, I listened to the metallic clunk of iron scaffolding bars. Several stall-holders had started to set up for the day. They would place wooden boards over the iron frame of their allocated market stall before pulling a colourful tarpaulin over the whole structure to protect their wares from the elements. This was London, after all, and rain was never far away.

Since I'd moved into a small one-bedroom apartment on Bath Terrace overlooking the busy marketplace, I had fallen in love with both it and the residents of the local community—even warming to Tumble Town itself—far more than I'd ever imagined I could. I'd always been a city girl, but for all of my working life as a detective with the Ministry of Witches Police Department, I'd lived on the 'right side', near Celestial Street, where the industrious and the good and the great gathered. In sharp contrast, Tumble Town was the wrong side of the tracks. An enormous secret borough of inner-city London, where paranormal rogues and reprobates of all clans, creeds and species congregated. Here they resided, rubbing shoulders with those they would generally never stomach outside of this place, and here they plied their wares and their skills … and anything else that would earn them sufficient money to survive.

Because survival was the most that many of these unfortunate creatures could hope for.

You didn't have to look hard—or be any kind of detective—to understand that the majority of residents in Tumble Town struggled to make ends meet. Being a detective—ex-MOWPD but now a private detective—I'd witnessed plenty of hardship for myself. The lack of a decent education and access to suitable housing exacerbated the struggling economy. That in turn led to desperation and, inevitably, a rise in crime.

But at least the high crime rates kept me in business.

Aware that my heart rate was dropping, I figured I'd jog around the market one more time, just to cool down before heading inside for a shower. I had a busy day ahead at Wonderland, my detective agency on Tudor Lane. We'd taken on half a dozen cases in the past week alone, and while for the most part they were relatively straightforward, I wanted to meet with the other members of my team to ensure everyone understood what they should be doing and the deadlines I'd put in place. Sharing information and keeping up to date with each other was important too. I'd worked in settings where the left hand didn't know what the right hand was doing. It was stressful. Inevitably it led to chaos and more work for everyone.

No. Now that I'd set myself up in private practice, planning and communication were my key values. Meanwhile, failure was not a word I allowed to exist in my vocabulary.

Lily, the flower girl, was setting up her baskets of colourful posies next to the fountain, a stripy orange cat threading through her ankles. She fluttered a hand at me. "Morning, Elise! It's going to be a glorious day!"

"It is!" I called, returning her wave. I liked Lily. She was younger than me, perhaps mid-twenties, and so full of warmth. Beautiful with it too. Petite, no more than five feet two, she had a glorious head of brown hair that flowed down her back. Today she was wearing it in one thick braid. It slipped over her shoulder as she bent forward to arrange her stock. She'd told me she could sit there for hours at a time, five or six days a week, and never have a single customer even though her flowers cost so little. How she didn't freeze to death in the inclement weather we often suffered, I honestly don't know. I made a mental note to refresh the flowers in the vase I kept on my mantelpiece. The poor girl had to keep the wolf from the door, after all.

"It's about time the sun shone!" I added, and set off at a jog, intending to exchange a few more pleasantries once I'd completed a slow circuit of the square. Dodging past a donkey pulling a cart laden with freshly carved wooden statues of various gods and goddesses, I carefully kept to the path. Most of Tumble Town was riddled with Victorian cobbled streets and lanes, which played havoc with my ankles if I ended up straying onto those.

I held my nose as I ran past Lemmy the butcher's stall. Some of the produce he had on display appeared highly dubious to me. Oddly coloured, weirdly shaped and reeking of corruption. I'd stuck to buying only fruit and vegetables on the market and buying meat and other consumables from the shops nearer Celestial Street, where the world was a slightly more civilised place and shops were monitored properly.

I'd be the first to deny being a lover of bureaucracy, but sometimes red tape can be a good thing. I mean … there's cutting corners and there's dying of food poisoning thanks to an unregulated and supremely dodgy butcher's stall on Peachstone Market, isn't there?

A slow lap of the marketplace only took me three to four minutes. I dawdled towards the end, distracted by a sudden avalanche of oranges rolling across the square in front of me.

"Oi!" A pack of feral kids, mainly boys, shot out in front of me between stalls, Bert the greengrocer hard on their heels. "You scabby blighters! I hope you get caned at school today!" He pulled up in front of me. There was no way he would catch them, given he was at least six times their age and a rather rotund gentleman.

"I don't think they have the cane at school anymore," I said, bending over to help him pick up his fruit.

"Don't they?" Bert grunted. "Well, they ought to bloomin' well bring it back!"

I gestured in the direction the kids had taken. "That lot probably don't even go to school, Bert."

"And therein lies the problem, Elise." Bert led the way back to his stall, where I carefully placed my oranges in his display. "In my day we were taught respect. Those little runts don't know the meaning of the word."

Sadly, that was quite likely to be true. I'd often thought the kids of Tumble Town were in training for a life of crime. This particular group were always hanging around the market, getting up to no good.

"Nothing that a clip round the ear wouldn't sort

out," Bert grumbled.

I smiled. "Don't get yourself arrested for child abuse though Bert, whatever you do."

He snorted. "What's the world coming to, eh?" He held out an orange. "'Ere, Elise? Want one of these? They're not damaged, just a bit mucky. You have to peel it anyway, unless you're one of those weirdos who eat the peel."

"I'm not." I reached out to take the orange from him. It was good and plump. "You're pulling my leg. I don't believe anyone eats orange peel. Bleugh!" I pulled a face. "Are you sure you want me to have this? I hate to eat your profits."

"It's a thank you for your help," Bert said. "And if you like it, you can come and buy half a dozen more at full price."

"It's a deal," I laughed. "You—"

I didn't get any further.

A shrill piercing scream cut off our conversation. I froze momentarily.

It came again.

A woman, close by.

My training kicked in. Run *towards* danger, not away from it. Take command of the situation. Offer assistance. I pelted back through the stalls in the direction of the scream. The woman had quietened down now, but I could tell from the movement of people, all heading for the same place, that I was on the right track. I emerged from the cover of the tarpaulin roofs with the fountain ahead of me. The crowd were gathering there.

I pushed my way through. "Make way," I called.

"Make way!" It was one of those times I wished I still had my warrant card, but the spectators parted ways easily enough. They were bystanders, not there to assist but to rubberneck. I broke through.

At first I couldn't see what the problem was. Lily sat with her back against the fountain, her pale blue eyes sparkling in the light, a serene expression on her face despite being the centre of all this attention. One of her baskets had been upturned, but the other was where it always was. I picked my way through the small posies of flowers, carefully bound with twine, towards the woman I guessed had raised the alarm. She held a yellow bouquet in one hand, a coin purse in her other.

"Everything alright?" I asked.

The woman tore her eyes away from Lily to stare at me, her lips moving, her breath huffing out in short erratic gasps. Shock, I decided. Reaching out, I placed my hand on her lower arm, seeking to reassure her.

"I-I just wanted to pay for m-my flowers," she managed.

"Sure." I turned my attention back to Lily, a tight knot of anxiety forming in my stomach. She'd remained in exactly the same position. I noticed the slight slump of her torso, the unblinking eyes.

No!

How could that be?

It had been six, maybe seven or eight minutes since I'd spoken to her. I was going to finish off our conversation now that I'd completed my cool-down lap.

"Lily?" I knelt next to her, one knee on the step, leaning forward to get a better look at her face. She was entirely relaxed, the lips slightly open. I reached out to check for a pulse in her neck. Her skin was warm to the touch. As I adjusted my finger, she slipped sideways. There was a collective gasp from the watching crowd. Dropping my orange, I caught her and gently lay her on the step, again checking for a pulse.

Nothing.

Lily the flower girl was dead.

But how?

I turned to the woman who had found her. "What happened?" I asked.

She drew in a shuddering breath. "I don't know. She was already like this. I didn't realise. I tried to give her my money and she just ... sat there."

I scanned Lily's body. No obvious sign of trauma. Despite the warmth of the day, she had been prepared for sitting out all day long. She was wearing a long woollen coat in dark brown with green plaid, which fitted at the top and was flared from the waist. An emerald—probably fake—brooch was pinned to the left lapel. Her long braid had fallen over her shoulder and become tangled. I gently teased the hair free and moved the thick plait away. There, an inch or so below the brooch, was a small dark stain. I dabbed at it with the tip of my finger and examined what I found.

Blood.

Fresh.

The customer, watching my examination of Lily, dropped her posy. Scared she would scream again, I smiled reassuringly up at her. "Do you have a phone?" I asked. I tended not to carry mine when I was running.

When she didn't immediately respond, I prompted her again. "A phone? Have you got one I can borrow?"

She shook her head, her face as grey as spoiled milk. Many people in Tumble Town didn't bother with new-fangled mod cons like smartphones. Witches and wizards had numerous alternative means at their disposal to use for communication in any case, but many people simply preferred to be 'off grid' so to speak.

To each their own, but that didn't particularly help me.

"I do!" A man stepped out of the crowd, holding some old brick that should have been put out to pasture in the early noughties.

"Would you mind?" I asked, reaching for it. I wanted to phone my old boss, DCI Monkton Wyld. I could have simply dialled 999, but then the call might have been put through to any division.

I didn't want to risk that. Okay, this might not be connected at all, but I had a gut feeling about this.

Lily had died in exactly the same way as Wizard Dodo. A small precise blade through the heart. A minimum of fuss and drama, a minimum of mess. She might have been sitting here for hours before anyone had noticed, had it not been for a woman deciding to buy a posy of flowers on her way through the market.

It might have been a coincidence.

Yeah, it might.

But I, still champing at the bit to find out exactly who had ordered Dodo dead, didn't believe in coincidences.

CHAPTER 2

"Larch, you and Boysie go around the stallholders and take statements." DCI Monkton Wyld was directing his team. In his mid-thirties, he was handsome in a clean and classical way, with his strong jaw, his warm eyes and neatly trimmed hair. "Someone must have seen something."

Behind his back, I pulled a face. Even if someone had seen something, they were unlikely to share it with the Ministry of Witches Police Department. The residents of Tumble Town operated to a code. Honour among thieves and all that. It was infuriating, but that's why experienced coppers, such as my now-deceased partner, DS Ezra Izax, had always cultivated a network of snitches.

Speaking of Snitch, 'my' little friend Bartholomew Rich, that is, I spotted him lurking at the back of the crowd of bystanders. He was a rancid little fellow—all lank hair and missing teeth—but I'd grown fond of him.

Wizard Dodo had been his friend—perhaps his only friend at one time—and after Dodo's death, Snitch had elected to assist my fledgling detective agency in our search to find the wizard's killer.

The thing is, we now knew exactly *who* had killed the elderly wizard: a detective ex-colleague of mine named Cerys Pritchard. She was currently languishing in the secure women's wing at Witchity Grubbs awaiting trial. The problem was the prosecution had yet to prove she was sufficiently fit to attend court so, inevitably, there had been one delay after another.

Her time would come. I meant to make sure of that.

People forget that there is more to a murder than the sensational headlines would have you believe. Each victim leaves an indelible mark on the people he or she knew. Okay, Wizard Dodo had been a curmudgeonly old rascal, but Snitch and my landlady, Hattie Dashery, had been genuinely fond of him. Plus, even hard-boiled detectives who think they've seen everything are affected by the cases they try to solve, so I figured I had a duty to ensure Cerys went down for a maximum life term.

There was also the small matter that Wizard Dodo had decided to haunt me, too.

I blamed Alfhild Daemonne for that! Until the proprietor of Whittle Inn had turned up in the guise of a goblin in my office—don't ask—I'd successfully evaded the knowledge that Dodo was still in residence. Now, increasingly, he made us more than aware of his presence.

Good goddess. The man never stopped moaning!

And he repeatedly asked me whether I'd found out who had murdered him, too. Knowing that Cerys had been the perpetrator did not satisfy him—or me for that matter—because I knew that someone else had instructed her to commit the murder.

The 'who' was a matter of conjecture. I'd been trying to figure it out for a few months now, all the while attending to the other cases the Wonderland Detective Agency had taken on.

Monkton returned his attention to me. "I'll need a statement from you as well, Liddell."

Of course he would. "No problem," I told him, but gestured down at my sportswear. "But can I at least go home and get changed? I'm due at the office for a meeting at nine—"

Monkton snuck a glance at his watch. "You're cutting it a little fine!"

"I'm aware of that." The crowd broke out into excited chatter as the pathology team arrived. Chief among them was Mickey O'Mahoney, instantly recognisable because of his bright red hair and huge build; he always caused a stir. He was accompanied by Ruby, his long-suffering assistant—the Laurel to his Hardy perhaps. Each of them carried a heavy toolbox, eager to get started.

I shuffled forward as Mickey leaned over Lily's body, an unconscious movement on my part. I desperately wanted to know what his initial thoughts were. Monkton held his arm up to stop me from going any further.

"I think you'll find this is our crime scene now, *ex*-DI Liddell," he said.

I folded my arms. "Come on," I begged. "I found the body! I'm the best detective you've got!"

"Correction. You're the best detective I *had*."

At least he was acknowledging that, I suppose. "You know, I'll find out what happened to her one way or the other," I griped. "You might as well keep it legal and make it easy for me."

"Is that an admission of illegal activities, ex-DI Liddell?" Monkton asked, clearly enjoying himself. "Do I have to contact internal affairs?"

"I can assure you all the business conducted by myself and DS Izax while employed by the MOWPD was legal and entirely above board," I told Monkton. All that I would admit to, anyway. I wasn't daft.

"I know you better than that, Elise," Monkton jibed. "You always find a way to get the information you want, one way or the other."

Grinning, I pointed at Mickey. "So, will you let me through?"

"On your bike, Liddell." Monkton shook his head.

Sighing, I stepped away. I needed to get to work, but Lily's death was going to bug me for days. "At least promise me you'll compare the manner of her death to Dodo's," I said.

"Your obsession with that case is just not healthy," Monkton replied. "You should drop it. We have the killer."

"You have *a* killer," I reminded him, my voice rising. "The Dodo case is bigger than you think." People were turning to look at me. I lowered my voice. In Tumble Town even the shadows have ears. You were playing a foolish game if you allowed everyone to know which cards you held.

"So you say."

Bless him. Monkton, as much as I loved him, could be annoying at times. I'd shared with him the information I had on the Labyrinthian Society, but he seemed oddly reluctant to pursue it. Part of me could understand this hesitancy, of course. We had virtually no leads. The secret organisation's activities had mainly dried up in the six weeks since the kidnapping of my assistant, Wootton Fitzpaine, had led to the exposure of the group's existence.

Wyld had alluded to being under pressure from his own boss to move on to other cases, but more than that, I fully suspected that Monkton had no desire to tread on the toes of the Dark Squad. The latter might know exactly what DCI Wyld's MOWPD murder squad were up to, but the same could not be said in reverse. The Dark Squad were well above Monkton's pay grade.

"At least bear it in mind?" I tried again.

He shrugged. I took that as a good sign; it wasn't an outright no. He might be a fool at times, but he wasn't stupid.

"And let me know." I was pushing my luck.

The scene of crime photographer had finished snapping general images, which meant that Mickey could touch the body. In order to get to it, he had to move one of the baskets of flowers. Monkton took it from him and had a cursory glance through the prettily arranged posies. "Such a shame."

Bert the greengrocer stepped forward. "I can take those from you, sir? Sell them on my stall. Forward the takings to Lily's family?"

"That's a lovely idea," I said. Knowing that Monkton would inevitably disagree, I nudged him. "Good thinking, boss." I added the final salute to appeal to his vanity. Monkton liked to feel he was in charge. At least nominally.

Monkton saw straight through it, of course, but give the man his due, he knew when to cut his losses. "Sure." He nodded at Bert. "Make sure you give a statement to one of my officers and let them know where they can find you."

"Will do, sir." Bert nodded and carried the basket of posies away. I watched him, reminding myself I should buy a bunch. I could do it on my way to the office after I'd showered and changed.

"That's a nice thing Bert's offering to do, isn't it?" I smiled at Monkton.

He sniffed. "There's a side to everyone in Tumble Town. You should be more alert to that than most. Too many game players and poker faces. I don't like it."

"Such a cynical view to take," I protested. I'd been living here long enough to know that simply wasn't the case. Not always.

"Says she." Monkton raised a quizzical eyebrow. "You're the one trying to link this case to the murder of Elryn Dodo. *Without* probable cause, I should add."

There was no reaching him. I exhaled in exasperation. "Just—"

"Ah!" Monkton lifted a finger. He considered the matter closed.

I pursed my lips and glared at him, sniffed loudly, then turned on my heel.

"Don't get involved, Elise," he called after me.

Too late.

I already was.

"I am so sorry!" I thundered up the stairs of 125 Tudor Lane and burst through the door to find Widow Lefferty waiting for me, sitting on the little corner sofa we'd placed as a holding area near the entrance. She was a tiny bird of a woman, like a little black-eyed wren. Her head twitched nervously when I held my hand out to shake hers. "Good morning, Widow Lefferty."

Ezra Izax—or rather his ghost—made a great show of looking at his wrist. "Don't worry," he told me, "Wootton has been looking after Widow Lefferty."

I spotted the mug of black liquid on the coffee table with a packet of Jaffa cakes by its side. The biscuits hadn't even been opened.

"Hope you don't mind?" Wootton waved a Jaffa cake at me. "I raided petty cash."

"And you bought *two* packets?" I narrowed my eyes at him. "We're not made of money."

"They were buy-one-get-one-free. It would have

been a shame to leave one packet languishing on the shelf, wouldn't it?"

Cheeky tyke.

"I suppose." I pointed at the mug in front of Widow Lefferty. "Have you brewed coffee?"

"I have." Wootton jumped to his feet. "I'll pour you one."

"It's fine, I'll get it. I'll take Widow Lefferty through to the back office, and we'll chat there." I knew my next appointment was scheduled to arrive at ten, and it would be best if they waited for me out here in the main office. The room out the back was a private place, perfect for seeing clients despite the little kitchen appearing slightly incongruous in the corner.

I gestured for Widow Lefferty to follow me through to the rear office. She shuffled slowly in my wake, glancing curiously at the sleeping form of Wizard Dodo slumped at my desk. I say *my* desk, but since he'd reappeared, he'd commandeered it on the grounds that it *used* to be his. It was a big, old-fashioned affair, crafted in oak with an extremely comfortable matching chair. For a while there, I had felt like the captain of my own ship, but now I'd had to move to the spare desk. This IKEA special had a chair on castors that were permanently wobbly. All that *and* I had to put up with Dodo's whinging all day long.

Unless he was asleep.

Fortunately, he slept a lot. Probably due to his grand age.

Speaking of age, Widow Lefferty had to be eighty if she was a day. Her face was lined by time, and her shoulders bent with osteoporosis, but still she kept on going, fighting to see justice for her husband who had been killed in an industrial accident over fifty years previously. She had tried countless times to see the business's owner—and then, after he'd passed away, his son—in court, but so far she had never succeeded.

I doubted, given the statute of limitations on such things, and the impossibility of finding evidence after so long, that I would be any more successful than previous private investigators had been, but there is no fail without try. I'd agreed that my agency would consider looking into the issue for her, and today was our first proper discussion.

After making Widow Lefferty comfortable, I popped my head back into the main office. "Wootton?" I called above the din of the ringing phone. "Are you busy?"

Wootton shuffled the half dozen files on his desk and reached for the phone. "Busier than I've ever been."

"When you get a second, could you—"

He held up a finger and picked up the receiver. "Good morning! Wonderland Detective Agency, Wootton Fitzpaine speaking. How may I help?" He nodded. "Absolutely. Yes. Yes. Would you mind holding for one second?" He pressed a button and directed his attention back to me. "Sorry, boss. You were saying?"

I stepped back into the bigger office. The phone on Ezra's desk had started to trill now, too. He didn't appear to be overly bothered about it. I knew him of old: he would happily let a phone ring out. It drove me nuts. I lifted the receiver and handed it over to him. It hung in the air between us and Ezra barked into it. "Izax!"

"What's all the noise?" Dodo had woken up. He glanced around the office, thoroughly bewildered by all the activity. "Oh, it's you lot! You're still here then?"

Ignoring Dodo and moving closer to Wootton, I asked, "Do you know Lily the flower girl who worked on Peachstone Market?"

He crinkled his nose. "Why would I know anything about flowers?"

"It's not the flowers I'm interested in. It's her."

He shrugged. "No."

"Well, see what you can find out." I turned away. "Please," I added as an afterthought.

"Any surname for me?"

"I don't know it, sorry." I paused, looking back at him.

He huffed. "Anything helpful I can use?"

"She's dead," I told him. "You could start there."

"Dead? Right." He wrote two words down on his pad. *Lily. Dead.*

"You have to use your initiative, lad," Dodo bellowed at Wootton. "She's testing you."

"I'm totally not." I frowned at the crabby old sausage. "That is literally all I know about her."

Dodo waved a hand, dismissing me, and addressed Wootton again. "I wouldn't trust that one. She keeps things close to her chest." He tapped his nose. "I'd watch her."

Tutting, I left them to it and returned to Widow Lefferty.

Ensconced in the back office, I surfaced for air just after midday. After back-to-back meetings with my new clients and far too much coffee, my head was ringing. Fortunately, the front office had lapsed into serenity in my absence. Ezra, his feet up on his desk, was contemplating a crossword while Dodo was snoring away contentedly, his whiskers twitching while he dreamed.

Only Wootton appeared occupied with agency matters. He was tapping his pencil against his forehead while scowling at his computer screen.

"Everything alright?" I asked, depositing three folders on his desk.

He absently reached for them. They contained the notes and information I had collated during my meetings this morning. The second two cases were relatively minor matters. A potential affair that needed uncovering and a lost dog named Bogey. I wouldn't want to be the owner of a lost dog, wandering the lanes of Tumble Town yelling, "Bogey! Bogey, come!"

Widow Lefferty was obviously a more difficult case altogether. The poor woman didn't have much money either.

"That flower girl you were on about?" Wootton said, without taking his eyes from the screen. "Her surname was Budd."

Bogey? Lily Budd? What was it with these daft names? "That's a good start," I said.

"You didn't mention she'd only died this morning."

Wootton pointed at his screen. "Details are only now emerging on *The Celestine Times* website."

I walked round to his side of the desk to peer over his shoulder. There wasn't much information. *Local Flower Seller Dead in Marketplace*, the headline read. Underneath, the article continued: *Police this morning are hunting a killer after the body of Lily Rose Budd was discovered next to the fountain in Peachstone Market. The MOWPD are appealing for witnesses to come forward. More details as we get them.*

"Well that's something, I suppose."

"Except it isn't." Wootton looked up at me. "I've done all the usual searches—and there's no such person as Lily Rose Budd." He clicked on a different window. "With no age to go on, I searched through the register of births, deaths and marriages. You said she was young. I figured that meant younger than you, Grandma, but if she had been a child you would have mentioned that. I searched all women born between fifteen and thirty-three years ago, and there's nothing."

"That's bizarre," I said. "There must be something in the Tumble Town parish records?"

"Not a thing." Wootton showed me the results of a third search. "Nada."

"I'm thinking she wasn't from Tumble Town." Snitch's distinctive weasely voice drifted out of the doorway, startling me.

I slapped my chest with the flat of my hand. "Crikey, Snitch! Do you mind? You scared me to death!"

"Sorry, DC Liddell." Snitch sounded contrite. He

could never remember I'd been a DI. I'd given up reminding him.

Wootton sniggered. "That's the perils of old age."

Whacking his arm with the back of my hand, I asked him, "Did *you* know he was there, then?"

Wootton laughed again and shook his head. "Nope. And I do usually hear people when they come through the front door downstairs, let alone climb this final flight of stairs. All that creaking. Given the age of this building, I'm surprised it doesn't fall down, to be honest."

"Don't say that!" I wasn't superstitious, but my mother was. She'd always drummed into me that you shouldn't say anything negative out loud. To utter words was to gift a thought to the universe. In my mother's mind, that had a sure-fire way of backfiring.

Ezra snorted. "Are you worried you'll be joining me in the afterlife sooner than anticipated, Elise?"

"I'm going nowhere," I growled. "You told me there were no vodka bars so I'm staying put right here." I narrowed my eyes at Snitch. "I saw you in Peachstone Market this morning. What were you up to?"

Snitch sidled in through the door and carefully surveyed the office, checking for anyone he didn't want to bump into, no doubt. "Not much. I heard on the grapevine that there'd been a murder. I was curious, that's all."

He spied the open box of Jaffa cakes on Wootton's desk. "Oh!" he cooed. "Them's orange, ain't they?"

Before Wootton could protest, I handed the box over

to Snitch, whose eyes lit up like stars. "Fank you, DC Liddell!"

"Sit down, Snitch, you're making the place look untidy." I took my own wobbly seat at the cheapo desk and surreptitiously pulled a notepad out of the drawer. "What makes you think that Lily wasn't from Tumble Town?"

Snitch extracted a round chocolate biscuit-come-cake from the plastic and delicately nibbled on the outer edge. Nibbling is hard to do when you have your front two upper teeth missing, so he used his incisors. It was captivating to watch. He swirled the tiny morsel of chocolate around his mouth and sighed in ecstasy. "Scrummy."

"Snitch?" I prompted.

He carefully placed the Jaffa cake pack on top of the box. "Oh right, yeah. So, I ain't heard much, if I'm honest, but the shadows were abuzz with the news. The thing is, Lily—or whatever her name is—she weren't a regular in the market until recently."

That was weird. She had fitted into the general daily life of the market as though she had been born to it and it was all she'd known. I'd had no idea she hadn't been in her place by the fountain day in and day out for donkey's years.

"How recently?"

"She turned up there about the same time you moved in," Snitch said, reaching for his Jaffa cake again. "Before that, no-one knows where she came from."

I exchanged glances with Ezra, spotting the tweak of interest from his left eyebrow. He shook his head, implicitly understanding what I was thinking. "It's not our case," he said quietly.

I thought back to the stab wound through Lily's heart. Dodo had fallen asleep again. He snored gently, his whiskers covering the hole in his own chest.

The universe was lining things up. Lily Rose Budd— not her real name—had arrived in Peachstone Market at the same time as I had. Her manner of death was the same as Dodo's.

Dang those coincidences!

"It is now," I said.

CHAPTER 3

Monkton groaned when he spotted me slinking around the police cordon. "I thought I'd got rid of you," he said.

"You'll never get rid of me," I told him cheerfully. Peachstone Market was a ten-to-twelve-minute walk from the agency. I'd excused myself from my fellows by explaining I'd left my lunch at home. I don't think they'd bought my excuse at all, but I was the boss, so they couldn't say anything.

Or something like that, I kidded myself.

"It is beginning to feel that way," Monkton agreed.

"You love me really." In one nifty movement I swung myself under the tape. Before Monkton could protest, I continued, "Nobody came to take my statement, so I thought I'd voluntarily pop back and let you do it yourself."

"Give us a chance, Liddell. We're still processing the scene," Monkton grumped. He hated being at the scene of a crime. He much preferred investigating the murder using old-fashioned means—questioning suspects, chasing culprits, doing the legwork—none of this hanging around waiting for forensics to do all the dirty work.

The problem nowadays was that forensic science solves far more crimes than beat officers do. I figured Monkton Wyld had been born into the wrong era.

I peered over his shoulder. Mickey and Ruby and a couple of their colleagues were packing up. Mortuary technicians were getting ready to move the body back to the pathology lab where Mickey would perform the post-mortem. I found these fascinating. Monkton was far less keen. No wonder he was grumpy if that was his next destination.

Monkton followed my gaze. "I know what you're thinking, and the answer is no."

"You know, I never knew you were a psychic," I told him. "I was just contemplating how long it's been since I've had a drink with all my buddies." I waved at Mickey and, peeling off his face mask, he walked towards us. "But it seems you don't want to join us. Never mind."

"Hey, trouble!" Mickey grinned. "Fancy meeting you here."

"I'm an important witness this time." I nodded, keeping my face serious. "I was here when the body was found."

"That's getting to be a habit of yours," Mickey said. He turned to Monkton. "We've done all we can do here. I'll accompany the body back to the lab and get stuck in."

Monkton snorted. "That's an unfortunate turn of phrase."

"I don't suppose you'll find much more than we already know," I chimed in. "Single stab wound to the chest with a thin implement. No other injuries. No defence wounds because she was caught by surprise ..."

"Alright, Quincy!" Mickey pretended to back off. "Trying to do me out of a job?"

"It's true though, isn't it? I'll bet a tenner."

"You're on," said Mickey. "If that's all I come up with at the post-mortem, you'll have earned it."

Monkton folded his arms and tutted. "Good job, Liddell."

I smirked. Now, one way or the other, I'd find out what the autopsy report said, wouldn't I?

"You can spend it on the first round for our big night out," Monkton continued. "Mickey will appreciate a chance to cut his losses."

"What big night out?" Mickey asked.

"Oh, haven't you arranged anything yet?" Monkton feigned surprise. "I was under the impression Liddell here had sorted out an evening of entertainment for us all. Just like the old days."

"First I've heard." Mickey shrugged. "I can't make tonight, anyhow. I'll be tied up. I've a backlog waiting for me as it is. Something like this comes in and I have to put a hold on everything else. You police guys always want everything yesterday." He wasn't complaining, merely making an observation.

I began to inch away, heading in the direction of the fountain. "We'll take a rain check then, yeah?"

"Where are you off to, Liddell?" Monkton asked.

Mickey reached out for Monkton before my old boss could come after me. "Can I run something by you?"

Making the most of the distraction, I hotfooted it over to the fountain where Lily was still lying. Her skin had paled now, her lips tinged with blue. Little plastic markers were dotted around her body, but there weren't many of them because there wasn't much evidence to gather. It was a peculiarly clean murder scene.

The only real thing of note was a run of plastic markers spreading in a slightly curved line away from the body. I leaned over to get a better look at what they were indicating. Drops of blood by the look of it. I traced the arc with my eyes and tried to envisage which exit the murderer had taken. Up one of the many side alleys that fed into the marketplace. That wouldn't be much help to me if I wanted to track him. I could tell by the gapping between blood drops that the murderer had been moving rapidly. Hardly surprising, considering what he'd done and how busy the market had been.

I checked my thought process. It may not have been a man. It had been Cerys who had killed Wizard Dodo after all. Perhaps the assailant had been a woman.

"Hey!" Monkton had shaken loose from Mickey.

I smiled at him. "Have you managed to find out her real name yet?"

"Real name?" His brow wrinkled.

"Come on," I said. "Lily Rose Budd? I'm not buying that."

"Stranger things have happened," Monkton answered, but I could see the cogs whirring away behind his eyes.

"Right!" I turned away with an air of finality. "Best crack on. Clients to see, cases to solve. You know how it is."

"Hmmm." Monkton narrowed his eyes. "Is that so?" He indicated the fountain where the technicians were preparing to carefully move Lily's body. "This isn't one of those cases though, is it Liddell?"

"Certainly not," I reassured him. "Only so much as it impinges on my investigation into the death of Wizard Dodo, or"—I pretended to think for a second—"if I thought for a second that I was implicated in some way, you know, given that I was one of the last people to see her alive and I phoned it in—"

"You're impossible," Monkton growled.

"I won't get in your way," I promised, and skipped off.

"What about that night out you promised?" Monkton called after me.

"I'll be in touch!" I shouted back, and slipped between a pair of stalls, one of which was flogging hand-thrown Azerbaijani pottery and the other selling hoods and hats suitable for every magickal persuasion.

I made my way to Bert's, knowing from previous conversations with him that his family had run a stall in the marketplace since time immemorial. He would know things. Useful stuff. His was one of three fruit and vegetable stalls on the market but even so, he was popular. His stall overflowed with luscious bright bounty.

Wasps hovered here and there, searching for illicit sugar, flies buzzed busily, hopeful of more rotten spoils. I could see Lily's basket arranged at the front, a hastily scrawled note half buried among the small bouquets of flowers, proclaiming: 'All proceeds to be past to Lily Rosebuds family. RIP! Donatuns greatfuly recieved.'

As usual, there was a short line of people waiting to be served: a young man with a huge bunch of bananas, another stallholder with a bag of cherries and a pair of tiny old ladies who might have been twins, one of them carrying a shopping bag, the other an umbrella despite the weather looking set to be fine most of the day.

Awww. That's dead cute, I thought, pondering whether they had always lived together. I couldn't imagine living with my sister. We'd drive each other to distraction.

I hovered behind them, slightly to the side, waiting to catch Bert's eye, while admiring the complicated swirls of their silver hair, braided identically and looped around the crown of their heads. They couldn't have been as much as five feet tall. I wondered how old they were and how long they had lived in Tumble Town. Like many of the older residents, they were wearing thick, fitted wool coats over long skirts. A typical dark witch's outfit, I'd come to realise over the past few months.

It was almost their turn to be served. One of them slid sideways, sneaking a tiny hand inside Lily's basket. Finding the action slightly odd, I frowned.

As though sensing my scrutiny, the other woman turned to examine me. Her black, birdlike eyes glittered. For some inexplicable reason, I had the sense she recognised me. The same could not be said for me. I'd never seen her before.

She cleared her throat. A harsh sound like a crow's caw. Her sister, without missing a beat, smoothly withdrew her empty hand from Lily's basket.

I ironed out my features, not wanting either of them to recognise my suspicion. A pair of petty thieves working in tandem, eh? "Lovely day for it, isn't it?" I said. I wasn't sure what 'it' actually referred to, but the traditional and decidedly English greeting seemed to cover all bases.

The first sister pressed her lips together and regarded me, not with malice exactly, but certainly with a chilly loathing.

"Yes ladies?" Bert had finished serving his fellow stallholder with her cherries and was turning his attention to the twins.

"Two swedes," the other twin said. The first one carried on staring at me.

"Is that everything?" Bert handed over a pair of creamy, purple-topped swedes, each the size of a skull.

The second twin thrust a number of coins at him and, without waiting for her change, pivoted neatly in place. Taking her sister's arm—and without making eye contact with me—she stood in place, biding her time.

The first twin cut her eyes at me. "Busybody," she spat. "We don't need your sort here."

Before I had a chance to respond, the pair were off, marching in step, as quick as you like.

"Ha." I stared after them. "Not so cute, after all."

"You alright, Elise?" Bert asked. "Did you want something?"

It would be churlish of me to refuse. I'd lost my orange in all the rigmarole this morning, so I selected two and handed them over. "I'll have a couple of onions, carrots and potatoes please," I told Bert, and he efficiently bagged several of each for me to take with me.

"What ya making, love?" he asked.

"A thin summer soup, I expect." I shrugged. "I'm good at soup. If I chuck it in the slow cooker, I don't burn it."

Bert huffed in amusement.

Seeing we were alone, albeit temporarily, I seized the opportunity. Nodding at Lily's basket of flowers, I asked, "Have the police taken your statement yet?"

"They were round 'ere, yeah. But I ain't got much to say to that lot."

As I'd thought. It would be hard for Monkton and his team to make any inroads in Peachstone Market. The residents were naturally suspicious of the police. It wouldn't matter whether it was Monkton or the Dark Squad—I had a feeling everyone would remain tight-lipped. I remembered those days well, coming over here from Celestial Street and expecting everyone to open up to me. Invariably, despite my most charming and cajoling manner, I could never get anywhere.

"Did you know Lily well?" I feigned indifference. Bert knew what I was, where I'd come from. Everyone did. But living locally, among the people of Peachstone Market, surely that made a difference?

It seemed it did.

He shook his head. "Nah. She's relatively new to Peachstone Market. Been here a few months. I mean, there's always been a flower seller on that pitch but yeah, she hadn't been here long, may the goddess bless her."

"So you didn't know that much about her?"

He thought for a moment. "Y'know, I'm not sure anyone did, actually. She was pleasant. A nice young lady, and she chatted to anyone and everyone …"

"But?" I could hear the hesitation in his voice.

"But maybe she was a bit of a light head."

What on earth was one of those? "A light head?"

"Yeah, y'know. All fluff and clouds and stuff. Liked to catch up on all the local gossip and not a lot else."

"Oh right! An airhead?"

"That's the one. One of them airheads, yeah." Bert swatted a wasp away and carefully straightened his plums. "I'm not bein' disparagin'. I liked her. I did."

"All the times I spoke to her, she did seem lovely," I agreed. He was right though. Now that I thought about it, I'd never exchanged more than pleasantries with her either. But was that so weird? We were acquaintances, on little more than affable nodding terms. Why should she have shared her life story with anyone?

"So sad." He pulled a chewed pencil from behind his ear and totted up my purchases on a paper bag. "Let's call it three quid."

Fortunately, I had my purse with me this time. I pulled out a fiver and waited for change. "Any idea where she lived?" I asked.

"No idea," Bert said, "but I imagine old Glossop will.

I'm intending to talk to him soon myself. See if he can help me track down her nearest and dearest so I can hand the flower money over."

"Glossop?"

"The market inspector. Manages everything hereabouts. He has a little office just over on the Sugar Row side of the market. Blink and you'll miss it."

"Thanks, Bert!"

"Catch you later."

I started to move away, but glancing at the basket of posies, I had another thought. "You're not keeping the money you take for the flowers in the basket, are you?"

"No, love. I'm keeping it safe behind 'ere with me." He lifted a little yoghurt pot, maybe a third full of change, silver and gold.

I handed back the two pound coins he had given me. "That's good. You wouldn't want anyone to pilfer it."

"You need eyes in the back of your head, I swear," Bert grumbled.

I thought about mentioning the silver-haired old lady twins but decided against it. They hadn't managed to get away with anything, so no harm done. It wouldn't do to poke every hornet's nest I came across.

Would it?

CHAPTER 4

Old Man Glossop inhabited the tiniest office I had ever seen—and believe me, there were a fair few of those in the Ministry of Witches building on Celestial Street. The majority of the buildings on the Sugar Row side of the market were eighteenth century, all pseudo-Greek pillars, austere and neo-classic, with the exception of this tall, late Victorian building in an elaborate art nouveau design. The now shabby exterior had surely once been beautiful, but it had been uncared for, like so much of Tumble Town, and now the woodwork around the windows was rotting and the paintwork had seen better days.

It was the windows on the bottom floor that quite took one's breath away: stunning stained-glass sections above clear glass that allowed browsers to check out the wares that each shop carried. I wandered past a robe shop, then a herbalist next door to a quill and stationery specialist. At the end of the row, I had to retrace my steps. My attention had been side-tracked by the glorious goodies for sale in a boutique, beautifully displayed, just as Hattie's window was, and I'd entirely missed the small office I'd been searching for.

The Peachstone Market Management Office—as a wooden sign leaning against the bottom of the building proclaimed in beautiful gold and green signwriting—took up little more than two door widths. Peering through the faded green glass, I could almost make out a man in dark clothing inside. From the outside, one could imagine that the inside would be a grand affair, but that most certainly was not the case. Pushing open the door, I stepped into a tiny cubbyhole of a room and promptly realised that there wasn't an adequate amount of space for me to be inside *and* to close the door.

On the other side of the counter—that just had to be as old as the building itself, judging by how worn and shiny the oak wood was—was a man, somewhere in his sixties. Slightly rotund and sporting a neat, dark moustache, he was wearing a crisp white shirt with a detachable collar and a charcoal waistcoat. Behind him, so close he might have speared himself on it had he stood up too swiftly, was a coat tree where his suit jacket and bowler hat were carefully hung.

He'd been tapping away on an old-fashioned typewriter, but now he looked up at me, his fingers poised above the keys. "May I be of assistance, madam?" he asked.

"DI Elise Liddell." I fished my private investigator's badge out of my pocket, praying he wouldn't take a good look at it and realise I was in no way affiliated with the police.

My luck was in. He stood up immediately, giving my credentials little more than a cursory glance, and yanked at the points of his waistcoat to pull it down and cover his stomach. He barely succeeded.

"How may I help?" he asked.

"You must have spoken to my colleagues earlier," I said.

His eyes shifted towards the window. He was edgy. Like his fellow Tumble Town residents, he didn't want to say too much.

"I don't have that much to ask you," I said, intent on putting him at ease. "Just a few quick questions." I jerked my thumb backwards. "You see, I live alone on Bath Terrace, and on a personal level"—I lowered my voice so that we became conspirators—"a couple of my neighbours have asked me if they have anything to worry about." I widened my eyes at him. "Well, being young, I suppose we all feel a little vulnerable."

"Of course, of course." Glossop nodded quickly, evidently empathising with my—and my fictitious young neighbours'—plight.

"So I was just wondering if you had anything to add, anything I could tell my co-residents?"

Glossop leaned over the counter. Up this close I realised he was older than I'd initially taken him for. He had covered his face with a thin layer of concealer or something similar, and his moustache had been coloured. His shirt, at first sight pristine, was a little grey from frequent washing, and he exuded a slight stink of cigars and Old Spice aftershave. "I'm so sorry," he said, his voice low, "I told your colleagues everything I could."

An interesting response. Telling Monkton and the team everything he *could* was not the same as telling them everything he *knew*.

"And they greatly appreciated your candour," I lied. "And of course, everyone on the market speaks so highly of you." I made a great show of putting away my ID. Official Elise was back in my bag. "I genuinely liked Lily. Used to chat with her after I'd finished my run in the morning."

"I've seen you running." Glossop nodded. "Whatever the weather."

I hid my excitement. He'd seen me. That meant that he spent time looking at people going past his window. He was paid to keep an eye on the market. I'd hazard he knew far more than he'd shared with my ex-colleagues.

"I'll miss her," I said. "Bert's organising a collection among the stallholders and selling her flowers. He'll give the proceeds to her family."

"He'll have a job to do that," Glossop told me.

"How so?"

"Like I told your colleagues, Lily claimed to have no next of kin." He pulled open a drawer from beneath the counter on the other side of the partition from me, instantly locating the file he was after. He pulled it out, opened it to the first page and turned it around so I could see. The form had been completed in beautiful handwriting, all flourishes and swirls. Lily's application form for a permit to work on the market.

"Is that Lily's handwriting?" I asked.

"No, no. Mine. I prefer to complete the details myself; that way I can read everything when I need to." He pointed at an illegible squiggle at the bottom. "I just ask people to sign when their application is filled out."

"So, no next of kin?" I mused on this.

"That's right. It causes a slight issue for the powers that be, as I'm supposed to have someone to call in case of emergencies."

Such as being murdered while harmlessly selling bunches of flowers.

"How did you get around that?" I asked.

"She gave me the number of an ex-colleague and close friend." He pointed at a scribble in red pen in the margin. Marcelle Blinksnap? There was a pseudonym if ever I'd heard one. I made a mental note of the number. Tumble Town 823824. Nice and simple.

"Did you call that number this morning?"

"It rang out." He shrugged.

"I see." I mulled over what he had told me. "Any idea what she did before she asked to sell flowers on the market?"

Glossop took the folder back from me. "Therein lies another small issue." He cleared his throat and lowered his voice once more. "She told me that she'd been employed as a florist on Tetris Alley."

A tiny bell began to clang in my head.

"But … ahem …" Glossop's cheeks reddened. "She was so persuasive. I didn't check until I'd already said she could work the pitch. She paid three months in advance. I didn't see what harm it could do."

"But?" I prompted him.

"It turned out there is no florist on Tetris Alley."

No. I couldn't recall seeing one, I thought, biting my lip. But I'd been more interested in scrutinising tattoo parlours the last time I'd been there.

"It didn't seem to matter. She continued to pay her rent on time and was personable. I didn't have any complaints about her from the other stallholders, or from customers. If they're happy, I'm happy. It certainly makes my job a lot easier."

"Thanks for your help," I said.

"Any time," Glossop retreated the few tiny steps to his desk and ancient typewriter, and I stepped backwards out of the door, pulling it closed behind me. Rummaging in my bag for my phone, I could feel Glossop's interest beyond the glass. I ducked sideways, out of sight, past the stationer's and down a little side alley, tapping in the number.

823824.

But something stopped me before I could press the call button. If I rang this number from my phone, the call would be traceable. Was that a good idea?

Probably not.

Better to find Snitch and get him to buy me some cheap burner phones.

Meanwhile, perhaps I'd take a walk over to Tetris Alley. Funny how all roads led in the same direction.

But why and what it all meant? That was a puzzle.

A puzzle of labyrinthian proportions.

CHAPTER 5

Perhaps it had been an act of bravado to assume I could stroll anywhere near Dead Man's Wharf and not feel a tad anxious. I'm not generally averse to walking into challenging situations, it's what I've trained my whole career for, after all, but there was just something about the east side of Tumble Town that caused my insides to quiver.

I'm not even sure what set the area apart from the rest of Tumble Town which, let's face it, was one massive community of people you didn't want to bump into on a dark night, but there was just something about Dead Man's Wharf—slimier, shadier, more unnerving— than anywhere else I'd ventured. And that, even in broad daylight!

But faint heart never caught foul murderers, right? I girded myself with an expresso from the same sandwich shop I'd patronised on a previous visit and slipped along the lanes and backstreets until I found myself at the top end of Tetris Alley. I paused to stare along the row of shops and houses leading down towards the quay and a number of warehouses at the very end. Everything here appeared to have been painted from one miserable colour pallet. Dark charcoal grey for the cobblestones, rusty brown and grey for the metalwork where shop signs might once have hung, battleship grey for many of the buildings. Blue grey or green grey for the paintwork. A grey sheen of dust and grime covered the windows; a window cleaner would be made for life if he chose to ply his trade down here.

A donkey, laden with heavy blankets, jangled as he clip-clopped slowly towards me. Even he was grey. I watched him come, driven relentlessly on by a man in robes, the hood pulled up and low over his forehead. I stepped to the side when they finally reached me, resisting the urge to reach out and pet the poor hard-working creature. Blinkered, he hardly noticed me, but his owner glanced at me as he passed … and just as quickly turned away. The first law of Tumble Town. Don't be seen to be seeing.

The jingling of the donkey's reins faded as I stepped into the alley. The shop nearest to me had long since been boarded up. I scrutinised the wooden board above the window, searching for some clue as to what it might once have sold, but the lettering was badly faded, the paint flaking away. The window of the shop next door had been lined inside with newspaper. Now badly yellowed, I could still make out the date on the top of the right-hand page of *The Celestine Times*, fourteen years previously. The next couple of shops had been converted into dwellings. Then came a newsagent's.

Miracle of miracles, it was still in business, although the light inside was so muted, it hardly encouraged browsing. I loitered outside, scanning the classifieds noticeboard. Someone looking for a lost parrot. Someone else advertising tarot classes. There were puppies available, kittens, rooms to let. A mage with an excess of gold feathers. Someone selling green dragon scales. Wand repairs ...

Glancing through the window, I spotted movement inside. Without further ado, I pushed open the door and stepped through. Instantly, the sweet, somewhat enticing scent of sugar and chocolate and tobacco reminded me of my childhood. The sales floor area was tiny, maybe eight feet square. There were counters on each side, piled high with chocolate bars and papers and magazines, with only the smallest of gaps for the proprietor to poke his head through.

Which he now did.

"Help ya?" Obviously a man of few words. I studied him, this man about my age. His pale, hairless face and bald head reminded me of a boiled egg. I couldn't see the rest of him, but I reckoned he was around five feet six or so, shorter than me.

"Do you have any mint humbugs?" I asked. They were Monkton's favourites and might help sweeten his temper.

He gave me the once-over, then sniffed. "Yeah. How many d'ya want?"

"Two hundred grammes, please."

"We don't do the new-fangled weights," the bald man said and indicated his scales. They looked like the ones hanging above the Old Bailey. A brass seesaw with bowls. "We strictly measure in ounces."

"Erm …" I performed a quick mental calculation and grasped at straws. "Half a pound then, please."

"Near enough." He twisted the cap off a jar of humbugs and dropped them through his fingers onto the scales before deftly switching out some bronze weights to make the scales hang evenly.

"Owt else?"

It had been a while since I'd visited a proper sweet shop. It would be nice to take some back for the office. "I'll have a quarter of rhubarb and custard, and …" I spied a bright jar of sour jelly worms. I loved sour jelly worms! "I'll have a half of those worms as well, please."

He measured everything out in no time, dropping the sweets into white paper bags and expertly twisting the corners so that nothing could fall out. The three neat packages were piled up together on the small counter.

"Is that it?" He sounded like a man who was perpetually fed up for no reason at all.

"Thank you, yes."

"Six pound," he said.

Six pounds! I fumbled for my purse, assuming he would only take cash, but he was already holding up a card machine. Not that olde worlde after all. I zapped my card and waited for the receipt.

He handed it to me. "So, what do you really want?"

Rumbled, eh?

Returning my card to my purse, I swapped it out for

my ID. "DI Elise Liddell, retired. I'm a private investigator."

"Good for you." The bald man folded his arms and pressed his lips together.

"How long have you had this shop?" I asked.

"Always." He held my gaze, his expression giving nothing away. "It's been in my family forever."

"So you've seen other businesses come and go, I assume?" I jerked my thumb in the direction back up Tetris Alley.

"Mostly go," he agreed. "Nothing much opens here."

"I'm looking for a florist."

He shook his head and shrugged. "Keep looking."

"You don't know of a florist on Tetris Alley?"

"I don't know anything."

I could hear the finality in his words; he wouldn't tell me anything. I reached for my sweets. That had been six pounds forked out for no good reason except to satisfy my own sweet tooth.

"There *was* a florist." The voice came out of nowhere and caught me by surprise.

"Grandad!" the bald man snapped.

"Oh hush, Lars. Move over." Lars stepped sideways, or he might have been pushed, I couldn't tell. His face in the gap was replaced by an older gentleman, equally as bald, but with white whiskers and long sideburns, and a few inches shorter than his grandson.

"Why do you want to know?" the old man asked.

"Someone used the florist as a job reference." I decided I might as well stick to the truth as far as possible. "I wanted to check it out."

45

The old man snorted. "I would have thought that anyone who'd ever worked there would be drawing a pension by now. Or pushing up daisies instead of *arranging* them." His laugh was a harsh bark. "Old Mother Mae's been dead herself now, this past thirty-odd—nay nearer forty—years I would imagine."

"Did someone carry it on after she died? Family?" That wasn't beyond the realms of possibility.

"Nah, she didn't have no-one."

"You said Old Mother Mae," I reminded him. Was I wrong to assume she'd been called mother because she was one?

Apparently so.

"She never had no kids. None as lived, anyhow. But she was an old woman when I was a lad, and all I remember is her bending over her blooms. She was permanently stooped over. Something to do with her back. We lads used to dare each other to kick her arse and run away, but the only kid that tried that—Gillan, he was called—came to a sad end falling down a well on Northcross Street. After that, we all minded our own business. Yeah. I always remember that. She hexed him, ya know?"

"So no family?" I prompted him.

"Nope. The florist closed when she passed away. For weeks after, you could see her flowers dying inside the shop. Wilting and drying up. Looking more dead every day. Eventually they just crumbled away to dust. Pretty much like she did, I imagine."

Nice.

"And there are no other florists on Tetris Alley?" I asked.

"None," Lars said.

"The nearest would be on Dead Man's Wharf, I'm supposin'," the old man said.

The door opened behind me and someone came in. I grabbed my sweets and stuffed them in my handbag. "Just one more quick question," I said. "Where exactly was Old Mother Mae's shop?"

Lars flicked his eyes towards the person who had come in behind me, but Grandad was already answering. "Carry on down 'ere. There's a burial place where the Tetris Alley intersects with Northcross Street. Her shop was the next one along."

"Thanks for your help," I said. Waving my bag of worms, I turned to leave but my progress was barred by the new customer, a tall, muscular man with reddy-blond wavy hair cascading to his waist, dressed in cowboy boots, a worn t-shirt and a leather gilet.

"Well, hel-lo darling," he said.

I started. The tattooist—if indeed that's what he genuinely was—from Wasted Youth Tattoos. Coming down here had been a risk, but I hadn't seriously entertained the possibility of bumping into him again. I'd made the assumption that if the Labyrinthians had become aware that the Dark Squad were onto them, they'd have gone to ground.

I'd been wrong. Or the man I'd thought of as 'the Viking', because of his looks, was a great deal more brazen than I'd imagined.

I nodded up at him. He had to be a good six inches taller than me. "Fancy meeting you here."

His smile was as wide as his face. He had good teeth. "Destiny." His eyes issued a challenge.

"Is that so?" I wondered whether he'd still think it was destiny when I had his butt arrested for … whatever I could eventually pin on it. "I have to be going. If you'll excuse me."

He didn't immediately move. I clenched my jaw. I wouldn't ask him twice.

Eventually he turned sideways, allowing me just enough space to pass. Without glancing back at Lars and his grandfather, I slipped out into the alley and hurried away in the direction Grandad had suggested, past the tattoo shop on my right, its door standing slightly ajar, issuing an invitation I had no intention of taking up.

I kept right on going, walking rapidly but never breaking into a run until I figured I'd put sufficient distance between myself and the Tumble Town Viking. Then and only then did I slip into the nearest doorway to catch my breath and think.

The Dark Squad had investigated the tattoo parlour but, according to Minsk, my rabbit friend and Dark Squad contact, they'd had no reason to take further action. There had been no evidence that anyone associated with the place had been involved in Wootton's abduction—or mine come to that. But to my mind, the coincidence was overwhelming. I'd been investigating the labyrinth tattoos and, while pursuing an avenue of enquiry, had been snatched when I'd left Wasted Youth.

The Viking, whatever his name was, had been involved somehow.

I risked taking a peep up the alley. He hadn't trailed me.

Huffing, I pulled my mobile out of my bag and rang the office. Wootton picked up on the seventh ring.

"Good afternoon, Wonderland Detective Agency. Woo—"

I cut him off. "It's me."

"Hey, Grandma. Where are you? Your next client arrived ten minutes ago."

Blast! I'd completely forgotten. "You'll have to reschedule," I said, kicking myself.

"Not to worry, Ezra is talking to them."

Double blast! I'd been hoping to elicit help from Ezra. Some backup, albeit of the ghostly kind, would have helped to put my mind at ease.

"Is Snitch there?" Snitch wasn't the kind of backup I had in mind, but at least he was streetwise.

"No. I'm assuming he went home to bed." In the background another phone began to ring. I could hear Wizard Dodo complaining about the noise.

"You couldn't try and reach him for me, please?"

"Sure."

"Tell him to call me on my mobile."

"Where are you?" Wootton asked again, his sixth sense kicking in.

"I'm—" Did I honestly want to tell him? I didn't want to run the risk of him coming down here after me. The last time he'd done that, we'd ended up in a whole heap of trouble. "I'm out investigating."

Nothing like stating the obvious.

"Right."

"Just have Snitch call me, okay? Or Ezra, if he finishes before you get hold of Snitch."

"Will do," Wootton replied, his voice cheerful as ever. "Thank you for calling the Wonderland Detective Agency. Have a great day!"

The phone bleeped and I found myself listening to dead air.

Fine!

Sneaking another look back up towards the newsagent's shop, I edged out and continued my way along the alley. Perhaps Viking Man had already finished whatever he was doing and had returned to attend to business at the tattoo shop? That was the best scenario.

I came to a crossroads. Had I turned left or right I would have found myself on Northcross Street, where once upon a time a poor little boy named Gillan had met a sad end. Northcross Burial Place was a small graveyard, chock-full of higgledy-piggledy stone markers. There was the odd statue—a gargoyle and something that looked like an eagle with fangs—but nothing particularly grandiose. Bordered on two sides by buildings, ivy climbed the walls, while one enormous yew tree cast shade over the eternally resting. These small graveyards cropped up all over the place in Tumble Town. Paranormal communities have so many gods and goddesses that they long ago opted to share burial space. Nowadays, people buried their dead wherever they could locally. It made paying their respects easier than venturing out of town to larger, more formal—and often too mundane—complexes.

Was Gillan buried here? Old Mother Mae?

I didn't take the time to look. Mae's old florist shop had been housed in a ramshackle building with a low roof. Or at least it was totally ramshackle now, although it may not have been quite so bad while she was alive. The roof was slate—grey, of course—but the building must once have had a thatch because I could see from the exposed wattle and daub how old it was. Now it bowed inwards. It wouldn't surprise me in the slightest if the whole dwelling collapsed while I stood and watched it.

More surprising, the windows were entirely intact. I cupped my hands around the edges of my face and tried to see inside but the glass was filthy. Grimacing, I swiped at the glass with the edge of my hand, only barely improving matters but allowing me to get a smidgen of a peep.

There were no lights on—I hadn't expected there to be—but natural light was entering the shop premises from somewhere. I could vaguely make out the shapes of a few sizable vases, buckets, a counter towards the rear, some shelves but not a lot else.

How peculiar that Lily Budd had claimed this as her previous employer when the shop had been closed for decades. How did she even know about its existence? That hadn't come out of the blue. There had to be some link between this place and Lily.

Ducking into the recess, I pushed against the old

door. Locked, obviously. I heaved my shoulder against it. It didn't give. Not even a little bit.

But that light was getting in from somewhere. A window or door at the rear, perhaps?

I heard footsteps heading towards me and pressed myself further into the recessed doorway, dropping my head and feigning indifference. It was hard for me to remain incognito, what with my hair and all. Given that robes with a hood would have helped, I don't know why I stubbornly refused to catch onto the idea.

A woman strolled past. Her eyes didn't so much as swivel towards me, but I knew that she knew I was there. My heart sped up a little as I recalled the woman with a headscarf on Providence Steps. When she only kept on walking, her feet, encased in hard wooden clogs, tapping loudly on the cobblestones, I breathed a little more easily.

The next problem was how to get around the back of the building. To the right, it was impossible. The building was the end terrace of a long row of cottage-shaped shops and houses. That left only the Northcross Burial Place.

I slid around the side of the shop, located the entrance and pushed at the rusty gate. It swung easily on its hinges despite its age and admitted me to what had initially seemed a random space to bury locals. There was an element of that, to be fair. I could see that some of the grave markers here had occupied the place for so long, the etching on their stones had been completely weathered away. Others were newer, standing out because of the lack of lichen covering the surface in its sticky powder. But surprisingly, I could pick out an element of orderliness to the layout too—some semblance of rows and columns, even if everyone was crowded together only feet below the surface.

Finding myself in the unenviable position of attempting to be both respectful and clandestine, there was nothing for it but to step on the dead as I hastened to make my way through the grounds, skirting the yew tree and grimacing as my boots sunk into the soft earth. I hated that sensation, as though the coffins below me had collapsed and the bony digits of the dead were reaching out to drag me down to sleep beside them for evermore.

A symptom of my overactive imagination, no doubt.

Ignoring the urge to loiter and read the inscriptions on the graves—perhaps seek out Gillan, who I now obviously felt connected to even though I hadn't been aware of his existence fifteen minutes ago—I found my way into the corner of the graveyard and scouted around for some secret entrance to Old Mother Mae's.

Nothing doing. Her shop joined the building to the left of me, right at the corner and, despite my best efforts to conduct a fingertip search through the thick ivy that clung to the old crumbling exterior, I couldn't find a way in through there. The wall was solid. Lamenting my broken nails, I realised there was nothing for it but to go all the way around the back.

Retracing my steps, hopping over graves and squeezing through the gravestones, I accidentally kicked over an old pottery vase. The remains of its stinking contents glugged out on the ground like thick, fetid brown blood. As I bent over to right it, I heard the sound of a can or something similarly tinny rolling over the cobblestones up Tetris Alley to my right in the direction of the newsagent's.

I froze.

It could be anybody, but ...

Remaining low to the ground, I carefully retreated until I could hide behind the yew tree. Peeking out, I waited.

And waited.

No footsteps. No jangling reins. No more rubbish blowing down the alley.

Elise's law, something Ezra had taught me long ago, was never to rush out of a hiding place. It would be too predictable to any potential foe. We all have a set amount of time we're prepared to wait before we move. Over the years, I'd become slightly cannier. I had the patience of a mundane saint. Waiting was my middle name.

So I took another few minutes to study my ruined nails and dig a little dirt out from beneath them, until eventually a crow above my head began to caw loudly, disturbing the peace. Anyone watching out for me would have looked in this direction. They might or might not have spotted me. Whatever. The game was up. I might as well move.

Strolling with purpose, I walked to the gate and exited the burial place. Glancing up and down Tetris Alley, I turned right into Northcross Street. The narrow passage took a dog-leg just ahead so that I couldn't see what—if anything—was heading my way, or any likely escape routes.

No matter, I was committed.

Breaking into a jog—part of me wanting to test if anyone was coming after me—I pushed on. Northcross Street turned out to be a narrow thoroughfare between parallel rows of mean little dwellings, rather like those in Packhorse Close, where the front doors practically opened onto each other and the only light came from lamps lit in the windows. Fortunately, we were a good few hours away from twilight, so I could still see where I was heading. Nine or ten houses past the kink in the road, I came upon a small passageway to the right. I hooked around and, stepping over and through piles of abandoned rubbish, eventually found myself in a confined space with tall fences surrounding me on three sides and several locked gates barring my way through.

Backyards?

Taking a moment to get my bearings, I grabbed the top of one fence and scrambled up to get a better look. Not backyards at all. Allotments! Tumble Town never failed to surprise me. I'd never have imagined that anyone would be trying to grow their own vegetables behind Tetris Alley, but here we were. There were only eight or so plots, and perhaps only half of those were well tended; the others had been left to go to weed. Hitching a leg over the fence, I heaved myself over, swearing loudly when my leather jacket snagged on an oversize nail, then landing in an ungainly heap in a pile of stinky compost.

Smashing!

Glad that no-one could see me, I righted myself and dusted myself down, dislodging bits of eggshell and mouldy apples … and worse. "For pity's sake," I grumbled aloud, shaking some gooey monstrosity off my thumb. Finally, giving it up as a bad job, I wiped my hands on my jeans and took a better look at my surroundings. There could be no mistaking Old Mother Mae's place. The roof was in a worse state from the rear than it had been at the front, sinking in the middle. Slates were clearly missing from several fair-sized areas, exposing the beams beneath.

The other houses, both those on Tetris Alley and those on Northcross Street, were in better shape, although not by much, and evidently still inhabited. Several chimneys were emitting thin trails of dark smoke, and I could see lights burning in some of the back windows.

I would need to be quick and careful.

Ducking again, I scampered towards Mae's place—from this rear angle, it looked more like a cottage than a shop—keeping close to the tall fence for as long as possible before ducking and diving between beanpoles and clumps of tall rhubarb until I reached the back door of the property.

This was where the light was coming in, I decided. The door had been forced open—some time ago, judging by the dullness of the splintered wood. If I'd wanted to, it wouldn't have taken much force to wrench it fully off its hinges. Poking my head inside, I scrutinised the interior.

This back room must once have been a kitchen-come-parlour-come-workroom. There were several tall store cupboards, now ransacked, built into the middle walls, a stove and a sink on the side wall and a wide wooden table in the centre. Pulling my standard issue police wand out of my bag—yes, yes … the one I should have returned months ago—I lit the tip and shone it upwards at the ceiling. Most of the plaster had crumbled away, exposing the beams of the floor above. I spotted several birds' nests in the room's ceiling beams. At least these feathery squatters were able to make use of Mae's old home.

Carefully stepping further inside, I moved slowly, taking care not to make too much noise or agitate anything. The last thing I wanted was the structure coming down on my head. It proved impossible not to crush the plaster underfoot, however. It crunched beneath the soles of my Doc Martens, and several pigeons flapped their wings in annoyance at my interrupting their peace. In the corner, tucked away, I spied a narrow door. Pulling it open, I found the stairs to the first floor. I shone my wand up the wooden staircase. I didn't like the look of it.

For now, I would continue my search down here.

There might once have been a door between this rear room and the shop itself but it had long since been removed, perhaps robbed for firewood or to replace a similar one in someone else's house. I stood behind the counter and surveyed the shop. It was, as Lars's grandad had suggested, as though time had paused. Everything remained exactly where it had on the last morning Mae had opened her shop.

The displays of vases were tiered. Large containers at floor level, buckets on the next tier, vases on the top. The grey husks of what had once been blooms had withered and dried out. Now the skeletons of roses and carnations gathered dust, spiders' webs hanging between them. The water must have turned rancid, and it would have stunk in here, but the smell, along with the water, had long since dissipated, and now only dust ticked my nose.

That dust lay thick on the old wooden counter. It hadn't been disturbed for years. Paper had been scattered all over the floor here, perhaps the wax wrappings that Mae had wrapped her bouquets in. There was ribbon too, great lengths of it, unreeled, draped over the shelves. I had no idea what colour it had once been, but now it was a deep unhappy grey.

The light changed, wobbling in my peripheral vision.

I took a smooth step backwards, retreating calmly into the kitchen. Someone, someone tall, was lurking at the front window, hands cupped around the top part of their face, squinting in, much as I had done not long before.

The Viking?

I remained still, knowing that he wouldn't be able to make out a great deal, but any sudden movement I made would alert him to my presence.

The shadow at the window finally went on his way.

The problem was, there was no way of knowing whether his way was my way.

Time to make myself scarce, perhaps.

Come to that, why hadn't Ezra called me back?

I reached into my bag, trying to locate my phone, but it didn't appear to be there. Sighing in exasperation, I checked again, then patted my pockets. I didn't have it on me.

Tch!

It must have dropped out somewhere. The burial place?

I backed up into the kitchen, intending to be on my way, but the door to the stairway stood open, as I'd left it, inviting me to take a look around upstairs. There had to be some reason why Lily Budd had chosen to list this place as her previous employer. It wasn't random. Maybe the answer was up there.

Swinging my bag back over my shoulder, I held my wand loosely in my right hand and used my left to steady myself up the narrow staircase. The wood of the risers was old, slightly squidgy, rotten perhaps. I rested my weight on the edges, fearful of my foot going through or the whole thing collapsing beneath me. Moving slowly, I made my way up, my heart in my mouth. My sixth sense was telling me to beat a hasty retreat, and yet on I went.

Pausing at the landing, breathing a sigh of relief, I glanced around. A front room and a back room. Both were bedrooms, both had been ransacked at some stage in the distant past, the few bits of furniture Mae had owned broken up and scattered around the floor. The remains of an old bedstead had been tipped against the old fireplace in the back room, as though to block that off, but apart from that there was nothing of interest.

The front room yielded a surprise, however. A hole in the roof, accessed by a ladder. The ladder itself was notable. It was modern—a lightweight aluminium affair —rather like a loft ladder, but not secured to anything above.

Gingerly, I tested my weight on the first rung. It would hold, no problem. I wasn't quite as sure about the floor beneath it. Time was running out though. I would take a quick look and then make a dash for it before it started to get dark. With that in mind, I climbed swiftly to the top and hoisted myself into the roof space.

Thanks to a small square window at the front, it was surprisingly light. Someone had taken time to lay boards across the joists and beams to ease passage. The space was tiny, not helped at all by the bow in the roof, and draughty thanks to the holes to the rear. There was evidence of more bird activity up here ... and little else.

But why go to the trouble to board the attic and buy a ladder for no reason? Bent double, I scuffled forwards to peer out of the window. This would have made a great spot to people watch. Had there been anyone to watch, that is.

As that thought crossed my mind, I heard a jangle of reins and the clip-clop of hooves. Another donkey, this one carrying shiny silver colanders and other kitchen equipment such as spoons and pans. He—I assumed he, but it might have been a she, I couldn't tell—clumped up the alley towards the newsagent's. I watched him go. By pressing my head to the glass, I could almost see the top of the narrow street.

I sat back and studied the area around the window. Noted the scuff marks on the sill. Leaning forward, I checked what I *could* see and what I *couldn't*. Not the newsagent's, because it was on the same side of the road as Old Mother Mae's.

But I *could* see Wasted Youth.

Interesting.

I sensed rather than heard movement downstairs. I couldn't tell you why. A change in pressure perhaps, or an alteration of the light. Gritting my teeth, I carefully moved away from the window towards the hole in the floor. What were my chances of hiding up here? Remote, I would have thought. If someone was after me, they would certainly search upstairs, and the ladder was a definite giveaway.

Up here, I'd be a sitting duck. There was nothing for it, therefore, but to climb down.

Clamping my wand between my teeth, I slipped a foot through the hole, feeling for the top rung. Inch by inch, I dropped down, trying to move quickly but silently, hating the cheap squeaks the aluminium made as I shifted my weight from foot to foot and hand to hand. Finally, the soles of my boots were on the floor. I remained frozen to the spot, my ears straining for the tiniest sound.

I could hear the slight breeze in the eaves above me. The creak of a door somewhere. The flutter of wings.

Had someone disturbed the pigeons? If so, that someone had to be in the kitchen.

I slipped out to the landing, holding my wand ready, studying the stairs. There was no way to get down there without making an awful lot of noise.

Kkkikkk.

The unmistakable sound of plaster being crushed underfoot.

That wasn't pigeons.

Cursing my rotten luck, I slid sideways into the back room. As I did so, I heard a clunk and a thump from the stairwell. Whoever was down there was on their way up.

I had no time to lose.

I hurried across to the small sash window and threw the catch. There was another thump behind me. I pulled at the window, trying to lift it, but it had stuck fast. The wood was rotten though. If I could find something to break it—

Thump!

I glanced around hurriedly. Just the bed. A length of wood—

Thump. Thump. Thump!

How far down to Old Mother Mae's backyard?

Thump!

Would I make it unharmed?

Thump! Thump!

No time!

I stepped back, intending to throw myself through the window. Praying that I wouldn't hurt myself, I covered my head and launched myself forward.

"Elise?"

The glass shattered around me, tinkling prettily,

catching the light, prisms lighting up my vision, my senses hyper-aware. The air, fresher out here than in the house, rushed at me, cool against my skin.

"Elise!"

A flash of light and the world began to slow down, the glass twirled around me instead of falling, and a huge up-gust of air caught me, a giant cushion that broke my fall. I landed lightly, on my back, but still hard enough to knock the breath out of me. Lying there, my hair a rainbow about my head, watching the shards of glass dance around tantalisingly out of reach, I spotted movement up at the broken window.

A white rabbit hopped onto the sill, came to the edge and peered down at me.

"Minsk?" I asked, my voice slightly hoarse. "What are you doing here?"

She wiggled her ears. "Saving your arse again, by the look of it."

CHAPTER 6

"Ma y arse wouldn't have needed saving if you hadn't been creeping around, all surreptitious and whatnot." I hauled myself to my feet, slightly surprised by the sudden jelly sensation in my elbows and knees. "Ooh, I've gone a bit wobbly."

"It's probably the adrenaline rush," Minsk said. "Do you normally dive through windows at the first hint of an intruder?"

"Not generally." I peered up at her. "But I thought I was trapped." I glanced around. "I could do with a sit-down."

"I'll come and join you. Do you want to catch me?" She teetered on the edge of the windowsill.

"No!" I held my hands up in a panic, willing myself not to drop her, but she only laughed. Her head disappeared from view, and I heard the sound of thumping as she hopped down the wooden staircase. A few moments later, there she was, standing beside me, cleaning her whiskers.

"It's filthy in there," she grumbled.

"What *are* you doing here?" I asked.

"I've been following you most of the morning. From a safe distance, naturally." She sat up on her haunches. "I was bored waiting for you, so I thought I'd come in and see what you were up to."

"You scared me half to death!" I scolded her. "Next time, maybe you could announce yourself in advance."

"Oh, you MOWPD lot. So fractious. I'll stick blues and twos on my forehead in future."

"You don't need to go that far. Just give me a shout!"

"Nee nar, nee nar."

I snorted. "Totally unnecessary, but thank you." Brushing some stray eggshell from the arm of my leather jacket, I asked, "You heard about the murder in Peachstone Market, then?"

"It came through on the wire this morning," Minsk replied. "I was curious."

"Lily Rose Budd," I told her. "A flower seller."

"A rather apt name." Minsk sounded as sceptical as I'd been.

"That didn't seem to matter when she was alive, but you're right. It does sound awfully like a pseudonym. Wootton was trying to do some background checks, but we weren't getting very far." I gestured at the back of Old Mother Mae's dwelling. "Our Lily gave this as a previous employer, but that's just not possible. Old Mother Mae has been dead for years."

"Did you find anything inside?" Minsk asked.

"Not a great deal—"

From inside the house came a clatter. Our heads

swivelled simultaneously towards the source of the noise. Downstairs. At the front of the shop.

Another *whumpf* noise.

I patted my pockets, looking for my wand.

"It sounds like someone's trying to get in," Minsk whispered.

"My wand," I hissed, "I must've dropped it when I jumped."

Crouching, I searched on the ground.

"When you fell, you mean." Minsk had a better vantage point, being lower to the ground, and immediately located where it had rolled beneath a discarded child's tricycle. I grabbed it and darted out of sight behind a fat wooden barrel full of slimy water.

I'd imagined that Minsk would join me, but when she didn't, I peered around the barrel, just in time to see her white bobble of a tail disappear in the direction of the back door.

"Minsk," I hissed. "Come back."

She ignored me and kept on going. I shuffled a little way out, staying low, trying to keep an eye on her. She disappeared inside the house.

Hesitating, I crawled towards the back door, but, hearing the noise of the door at the front finally being opened, I pressed my back against the wall and strained my ears to hear what was happening.

"When was the last time anyone was in here?" one voice was asking. I didn't recognise whoever it was.

"A while, I guess." Now *that* voice I did know. The Viking. "You sure she came in here?"

"She was poking around. Lars told me she was extremely interested in the florist."

"Why would she be, though?" the Viking asked. "This place has been locked up for years."

There was a crash, followed by a smash. Someone had knocked a vase over, whether accidentally or on purpose, I couldn't tell.

"Careful, Blakely." The Viking sounded annoyed.

"As if it makes any bleedin' difference." Blakely, the first voice, sounded completely exasperated.

"No-one's been here," the Viking said. "The nosy detective isn't here—"

"I just want to check it out. Lucky for me Lars had a key."

"Wasn't it." The Viking sounded oddly unconvinced.

A faint sound of broken pottery being piled up. What a weird thing to do, clean up after yourself in an abandoned building.

"His father was custodian of the building until a relative could be found," Blakely was saying. "But they ain't found no-one. After all these years it might as well be burned to the ground. I'm sure you could pay someone to do that for you, if you wanted to."

"Why would I want that?" the Viking asked. "Live and let live."

"I've considered it," Blakely said, ignoring that.

"I wouldn't." The Viking was firm. "You know what fires are like in this part of town. They can take out a whole row of terraces in less time than it takes to drink a beer. I wouldn't risk it."

The voices were closer now. In the kitchen, perhaps?

Where are you, Minsk?

"What are you going to do if you find this detective?" I heard a note of glee in Blakely's voice.

"Nothing," the Viking told him. "Don't worry. I just want a little chat."

Hmpf. Likely story.

"This is the door to the stairs. Should I check up there?" Blakely asked. Was that reluctance I could hear?

"Nah." The Viking sounded as though he were moving around the kitchen, opening drawers and cupboards. "She's not here."

From behind me somewhere came the sound of my mobile ringing. Some generic biddley-dingley-bomp tone that I'd never changed.

No!

All movement in the kitchen ceased.

I held my breath.

"Do you hear that?" Blakely asked.

"I do."

Suddenly a streak of white flashed by my face. "Elise!" Minsk shouted, "Run!"

I didn't need telling twice. I launched myself from my hiding place and sped after her, all need for secrecy gone. I sprinted for the wall, deftly jumping over vegetable patches and abandoned household goods as I went, Minsk always outpacing me.

"Hey!"

I risked a glance behind me.

The Viking had tracked Minsk out of Mae's house and attempted to chase after us, but he was no runner—that much was evident. Blakely didn't even try. He was silhouetted against the doorway meaning I couldn't see his face. I didn't hang around though. I had no desire for the Viking to catch up with me and have his 'little chat'.

My mobile phone had stopped ringing by the time I reached the compost patch. I scooped it up, worms and dead flowers and mouldy bread and all, and stuffed it in my pocket. Clambering onto the heap, I took a wild jump and clutched at the top of the fence, heaving myself up, using my feet to help me scramble over.

There was no handy compost pile on the other side to break my fall this time, and no rabbit magick to cushion me. I landed hard enough to jar my teeth.

Of Minsk, there was no sign.

"Minsk?" I hissed. "Minsk?"

"I'm still on this side, Elise." Her voice carried over to me.

Oh no! I should have—

"I'm fine," she reassured me. "Let's split up. That seems to be the best idea, seeing as we already have."

"Are you sure?" I contemplated climbing back over the fence, but the Viking had to be hot on our heels by now.

"Absolutely. I'll meet you back at Wonderland."

"Okay."

"Minsk out." There was a rustle and a scuffle, and I was left staring at a spot on the fence where I imagined she had been standing.

"Oh, Detective?" The Viking's wheedling voice threaded through the air.

I had to go.

Wasting no time, I hastened down the alley back to Northcross Street, my knuckles rubbing on the rough surface of the walls on either side of the tight passageway. The only question was whether to head for Tetris Alley, which I vaguely knew, and thereby run the risk of running into the Viking and his friends, or take Northcross Street, which I didn't know at all.

I didn't have a great deal of choice, did I?

CHAPTER 7

The light was starting to fail—not because it was late, but because this is how it was in Tumble Town, where all the crooked old houses were so close to each other, they made it difficult for the sun to penetrate the tiny alleys and passageways. As soon as that golden orb in the sky had sunk below the artificial horizon of uneven roofs, the gas streetlamps would blink on and night would suddenly descend.

I'd grown more accustomed to the earlier dusk in Tumble Town, but even so, the thought of having to navigate through the rabbit warren of back alleys in the general vicinity of Dead Man's Wharf, picking my way towards Tudor Lane, was not an appealing one.

The first trick? Not to panic.

I jogged along Northcross Street until I figured I'd managed to put a decent amount of distance between me, the Viking and Blakely, before pulling into a doorway and catching my breath while I considered my bearings. Dead Man's Wharf was due north, Tetris Alley to the east. If I—

"If I were you, I wouldn't hang around."

An old woman's voice drifted out of the shadows, papery thin, a rustle on a cool breeze, so close it startled me.

I caught my breath. "Who's there?"

"Who's there?" another voice asked. "Who is anywhere?"

I laughed nervily. Shadow People. That's all. Harmless.

As far as I knew.

"Who indeed? Who indeed?" came the third voice.

They were surrounding me. Regulating my breathing in an attempt to soothe the rapid beating of my heart, I scrutinised the shadows. Shapes melted in and out, but they had no definite form and absolutely no substance.

"You can run—"

"—but you can't hide."

Male voices. Female voices. It was hard to distinguish between them, and yet I could tell there were many of them.

I had the vague sensation of icy cold fingertips stroking my cheek. I shivered.

"But you *should* run—" The first voice, I decided. The old woman.

"Why?" I asked.

"Because *they* are coming," she said, her tone oddly sympathetic.

"Don't let them catch you," another voice beseeched me.

"Don't!"

"Don't!"

The chorus of wails was unnerving. I bolted out from the safety of the doorway and took to my heels once more, following Northcross Street around every bend, desperately seeking some left-hand turn that would take me south, back in the direction of Celestial Street. The cobbles and uneven ground made it hard going, and once or twice I turned a heel.

When I paused to massage my ankle and catch a breath, a whisper from a doorway urged me on. "Run!"

When I didn't immediately pick up the pace, something screeched in my ear. "Faster!"

As I sped on, my chest beginning to hitch, I began to panic. I couldn't keep this up. For sure, I liked an early morning jog, but this was something else. The pace, the windiness of the lane, the distance—

I slid to a stop and flopped my head down over my knees to give myself a chance to breathe and quieten my anxiety.

"Don't stop!"

"They're coming!"

"Run!"

"RUN!"

"No!" I screamed back. But at what? At whom?

There was silence. A light flared in a window to the side of me, the occupant of the nearest house lighting their lamps. I slunk sideways and wedged myself into another doorway, disturbing a sleeping dog. It cowered from me before slinking warily away, glancing back once or twice, its eyes reproachful.

A hiss. "Run."

"No," I repeated, more quietly, swallowing my rising alarm.

"But—"

"Wait," I told the voices. "Just wait a second!"

My eyes flicked left and right. What was going on here?

There were titters. "Wait, she says."

"Like she 'as all the time in the world!"

"We've got time. *We* don't mind waiting."

How far had I travelled? How long was Northcross Street? Surely there had to be a turning somewhere. I hadn't seen one on either side. Had I been going so fast that I'd missed them?

I laughed in realisation. "Magick."

"Maaaa-jick!" A mocking voice.

"Majik!" Jeers and titters.

A road that went nowhere. Was that possible? Could I get out of it somehow? Find the end of it? Locate reality? Or what amounted to my reality?

"You'd better run." It was the old woman again.

"Run where?" I addressed her invisible presence. "Where? How?"

"They're coming," she said. "Hurry!"

Were these Shadow People in league with the Viking somehow? What if I chose not to run anymore? What if I stayed right where I was?

A face lunged out of the shadows, a head twice the size of anything human. An old woman. Her lips were drawn back in a painful rictus of a smile, revealing teeth as black as the Devil's nutting bag. Her eyes—*oh hell, her eyes were missing!*—two empty voids in a face as old as time, the skin leathery and creased, criss-crossed with fine lines, a spider web of a life well lived.

"RUN!" she bellowed, and her breath was a fetid furnace of death.

I shrieked and ducked, losing my balance and almost falling.

Hands reached for me, tugging at my jacket and my hair. I beat at them—not that there was anything to see—then lunged free, catapulting down the lane, away from Tetris Alley, away from the Shadow People.

Just away!

But now I sensed I had company. If I took a moment to peer back the way I had come, I would spot the change of light as someone loomed behind me ... and yet ... there was no-one to see. In the quieter moments between my own ragged breaths, I began to hear foot-steps, keeping pace with my own, the occasional tap as a sole caught a cobblestone in a certain way, or a rasp as clothing brushed against the rough stone or brickwork of the walls.

It sounded so close.

I kept on going.

Every now and then, light would spill from a build-ing, and I would glance sideways, hoping for assistance. What if I knocked on a door? Would anyone come to my aid? But oftentimes, those windows would show me a face devoid of expression or a house seemingly empty. Most often, the curtains would be yanked closed, and I would be abandoned to my fate.

Abandoned out here.

With whatever was hunting me.

Because now I was certain that something *was* hunting me. Perhaps not the Viking, but something.

I was running out of energy. It had been a long day and I hadn't had much to eat or drink. Whatever was coming after me had more stamina than I and could match me pace for pace. If I slowed, so did it. If I sped up, it did too.

I couldn't go on like this forever.

But the second I pulled up, the Shadow People were at me again. Pinching, punching, jostling me, urging me to move, begging me to run. It was hard to know whose side they were on. Confused, I would flail this way and that until the cold clamminess of their invisible fingers would become too much to bear and I would stumble away.

There has to be a way out of this, there has to be! I lurched forward, my legs as heavy as lead. Above my head, a gas lamp spluttered out as I reached it. Taking a welcome break, I paused, staring up at it, watching it swing slowly on its bracket. What could have made it move that way? I couldn't feel the slightest hint of a breeze.

A rumble behind me, like an enormous stone had been rolled away from the entrance of a cave.

I turned. *What was that?*

I could distinctly hear the tap of shoes. Two pairs of

shoes. Two people walking in unison at an even pace. Unhurried.

My bowels turned to ice.

The cool nature of their approach, the certainty inherent within their stride? Of everything I'd encountered so far, this was the most chilling.

I lifted my wand. "Get me out of this!" I begged it, but what could it do? What magick did I need? A portal? A squadron of my ex-colleagues to come to my rescue? I was a police officer. My magick was limited.

Another lamp spluttered and died. I turned back, facing the direction I had previously been moving in. One by one, the lights at the windows were being turned out. It was a domino effect, and it scared the blazes out of me.

I stumbled forwards, picking up speed, trying to move into the light—but every time a light was in reach, it too died. "Please, please," I implored, keeping my voice quiet, stupidly not wanting to alert the people— who already knew precisely where I was—to where I was.

I aimed my wand at a bracket and the lamp that hung uselessly above my head. "*Illuminate!*" I ordered. I would create my own light.

There was a splutter, as though someone had lit a match, and then a flare. It glowed softly—not the illumination I would expect it to give off, but something nonetheless—and in that ghost of a light, I finally spotted a left turn. My heart leapt. Without further consideration, I dived around the corner and ran—

Straight to the end of a tiny cul-de-sac, three houses on each side of me and two dead ahead.

I stood in the centre of the tiny circle, two tall Victorian lamp posts casting their light over my surroundings. But, as I stared around at the neat buildings, first one lamp and then the other fizzled out.

Behind me, the sound of approaching footsteps came relentlessly on, slightly speeding up as they loomed in on me.

My chin dropped. This couldn't be happening.

I was trapped.

CHAPTER 8

I could imagine myself, how I must look, paralysed
by indecision, defeated and waiting for whatever
nightmare was heading my way, and I didn't like
it. Anger started to build in my chest. I inhaled and
straightened my back. There was no way I'd be taken
without a fight. I lurched sideways and hammered on
the nearest doorway. "Hey!" I shouted. "Hey! Open up!"

There was no response, not that I expected one.
Undaunted, I moved to the next house, and then the
third. I couldn't sense movement inside any of them,
although they all looked lived-in. I smacked hard on
each front door with my open palm, making as much
noise as possible.

Where were the Shadow People now? Didn't they
have any more advice to offer? Didn't they have any
friends who could cajole the residents here into
opening their rotten doors?

The sound of footsteps in the alley behind me had

slowed. They weren't in a rush. What did they have to lose? I couldn't go anywhere. They had me cornered.

Moving to the next house I slapped on the wooden door much as I had before, but as I did so, I experienced the peculiar feeling of déjà vu. Didn't I know this house?

That seemed unlikely. I'd never been in this part of Tumble Town before, so why did it look familiar? Forgetting about the people chasing me, I stepped back and studied it.

The number on the door said sixty-seven.

How could a cul-de-sac this small have such a number? There were only half a dozen houses. It was difficult to tell the colour of the door in the dim light, but I had a sneaking suspicion it was green. I swivelled to stare at the window. Thick net curtains hung down, masking anyone who might have been staring out at me but, what was that? A glint of light. It moved. Firelight?

That was good news. Someone was inside!

I slammed my hand against the wood of the door once more, desperate to be heard. "Hello? Hello?"

The scratching of a chain on the other side sent my spirit soaring. *Yes, yes, yes, yes, yes!*

A key turned slowly—oh so slowly—and the door was pulled open, just a crack. On the other side, a short, bewhiskered old gentleman stared out at me. The one eye I could see glared at me, suspicion and distrust rooted there.

"I need your help," I pleaded. "Please let me in!"

The already minuscule crack shrank to a slither. I forced my knee against the wood and leaned into it with all my strength.

"I'm begging you," I told the fraction of an eye and smidgen of beard that I could see. "It's a matter of life or death." When that entreaty didn't immediately work, I added, "Or at least call the police for me!"

"The police? I hold no truck with their kind."

The grumpy voice was instantly recognisable. "Wizard Gambol?"

"Go away."

"Glyrk Gambol?" I could hardly contain my astonishment. "Open this door up right now!"

"Shan't!"

Shooting a worried look over my shoulder, I slapped my hand against the wood so hard, the shock of it travelled all the way up to my elbow. "Open. The. DOOR!"

"Oh, by all that's green," he grumbled, but finally—finally—he threw it open and I fell forwards into his hallway, landing painfully on my knees.

"Close it! Close it!" I shouted, twisting onto my rump and pushing myself to my feet.

He crossed his arms over his chest. "Open it! Close it! You need to make your mind up, missis. This isn't a hotel—"

"Close it!" I yelped, springing forward and slamming myself against it. The front of the house shook, the windows rattling in their frames. "Lock! Lock!" I spluttered, entirely incapable of forming coherent sentences.

"Good goblin gods!" Gambol muttered. He produced his wand and aimed it at the door. "*Alibi locate!*" A thin green string of sparkling energy pulsed from the tip and wedged itself in the keyhole. The floor shuddered slightly. The elderly wizard nodded once, satisfied. "There."

Hovering close to the door, I leaned forward to listen for the footsteps to close in, waiting for the people following me to begin pounding on the door. I wasn't out of the woods yet! Would Gambol give me up to them?

"I suppose you'll be wanting tea?"

"Tea?" I asked, stupidly.

"It's an aromatic beverage created from the dried leaves of—"

"I know what tea is!" I turned back to the door. I couldn't hear anything or anyone. Perhaps the wizard's house had impressive inbuilt sound insulation. It was a shame Gambol didn't have a peephole of some kind.

"You pour hot water over the—" Wizard Gambol was still lecturing me about tea.

"Is there a back entrance?" I asked, trying not to listen to him. He was being a smartarse. "A back door?"

"It's delicious," he finished. "Especially the Goblin Gunpowder variety."

I rounded on him in exasperation. Couldn't he tell my life was in danger?

Gambol shrugged. "But of course, you know that because you had it the last time you came a-calling."

He did remember me, then. "There are people out there coming after me," I tried to explain. "There's no telling what they'll do if they get hold of me."

"Oh, I'm confident there's some telling of what they'll do." The wizard wrinkled his nose. Surely he wasn't *amused*?

"This isn't a joke, Wizard Gambol!"

"Nuh-yeh," he exclaimed, not so much a word as a noise. "I never said it was, and you can't say I did. Now, were you wanting tea or not?" He swivelled and clomped through into his kitchen at the end of the hallway.

Perplexed, exhausted, shell-shocked if I'm honest, I traipsed after him.

"You could at least take those huge clodhoppers off," he whinged, referring to my boots. He had a thing about people not wearing outdoor footwear in his house. Fair enough, I suppose.

"I might need to make a quick getaway," I told him, pausing at the threshold and glancing in. So this was what a wizard's kitchen looked like, was it? A wide range dominated one end of the kitchen, blacked to perfection. A fire burned behind iron doors, and a kettle, settled on an iron plate, steamed above it. The furniture and fittings were wrought from reclaimed wood and old Victorian tiles. The cabinets had loops of knotted rope that enabled him to open the doors easily. All of the units and countertops had been purposefully made for him, given his short stature. If I'd been preparing meals here, it would have given me backache.

From all appearances, it did look as though Wizard Gambol liked to cook—there were storage jars and tins on shelves for pasta, rice, flour and other sundries—but he must also have concocted other things here, because he had a workbench littered with herbs and potion bottles and some rather garish orange liquid in a jug.

He lifted a teapot down from a shelf, pretty polka

dots and somewhat out of character for him—something he kept for guests, perhaps.

"You fret too much," he said, reaching for a tin canister speckled with age.

The floor wobbled again. Steadying myself against the wall, I asked, "What *is* that? Why is your house shuddering that way?"

"It's just settling. Nothing to worry about."

"It feels like a minor earthquake." I stole a cautious look at the front door. Nobody was knocking. There didn't seem to be any kind of fuss and bother outside. Had they given up?

"If you're going to join me in the front room, I'm going to have to insist you remove your boots." Gambol was spooning several tablespoons of inky black tea leaves into his teapot. "I don't want the outside to contaminate my good rugs."

This whole situation was surreal. I opened my mouth to protest, then closed it again. If I was going to take shelter in here, the least I could do was agree.

I walked back to the front door, leaned against it once more and strained to hear. Still nothing. Not the slightest noise. Not a dog barking. Not a bird twittering. The green bobble of energy circulated in the keyhole, shooting out tiny sparks. Leaning over, I unlaced my boots and padded back to Gambol in my socks.

He ushered me into the front room, where a healthy fire burned in the grate, and set the tray on a small table. I stared around, thoroughly baffled. Everything about this room was a replica of the one he'd occupied previously, but that had been a small house in Packhorse Close, over a mile from here. His chair and sofa, the photographs in frames, even the wallpaper was the same.

How could that be?

"Sit down, sit down," Gambol moaned. "You're creating a draught."

Speechless, I took the same seat I had before.

"And I can't bear a breezy house."

I glanced over at the window. The thick net curtains prevented me from seeing outside. I hoped they also barred anyone walking past from peeking inside. I could only imagine that the Viking—or whoever had chased me through the streets of East Tumble Town— hadn't witnessed me entering this house, otherwise wouldn't they have tried to come after me?

But would they be waiting for me when I left? I should phone the office, get someone to come and meet me.

Fishing my mobile out of my pocket, guiltily shaking off a bit of muck that had congealed to it in the compost heap, I touched the screen to wake it up.

"I wouldn't bother," Wizard Gambol announced. "That won't work here."

He was right. I couldn't get a signal. "Why won't it work?" I frowned. "My network is pretty good in Tumble Town."

"I block the signals," Gambol told me, sniffing. "Can't be doing with none of this modern communication. It's all a nonsense. Back in my day we didn't need all that."

"What do you mean, 'back in my day'? *This* is your day," I told him, placing my now useless mobile on the coffee table between us. "You're still alive, aren't you?" I double-checked. He looked pretty alive to me. Not dead like Ezra. Or Dodo. He had none of their transparency, nor did he have their ability to walk through walls or hover just above the floor.

"Of course I'm still alive! I wouldn't be though, if you'd had your way. You nearly gave me a cardiac arrest banging on my door like that and forcing entry."

"I didn't force entry," I protested. "You *voluntarily* opened the door."

"Only so it wouldn't smack me in the face when you bulldozed your way in."

That shut me up. There was every chance I would have forced my way in if even a few more seconds had elapsed. I had been desperate, after all.

"It's a coincidence you being here." I changed the subject. "And me bumping into you again."

"No such thing as coincidence, ex-detective Liddell."

He definitely remembered who I was. "I'm still a detective. Just not with the—"

"Ministry of Witches." He waved a fat hairy hand at me, his nails long and claw-like. Goblin hands. I glanced at a photo on the wall behind his head. Black and white. I imagined it was an image of him graduating from an Academy of Magick. He was flanked either side by his parents. His father, a goblin, was much shorter than both him and his mother, a tall, skinny witch with a hooked nose and beady eyes.

"They've both been gone a long, long time," he said softly, not turning his head. I could hear regret in his voice. He missed them. It was the first time I'd witnessed vulnerability in the little goblin wizard.

I felt a pang of sympathy for him. "I'm sorry."

"Not your fault, is it?" he griped, reverting to type. "We all die."

I didn't mind him snapping at me. I sensed that he did so to cover the discomfort he experienced at displaying even a modicum of his grief in public. It was something I'd often seen over the years while inter-viewing both suspects and witnesses. In the ensuing silence, I twitched in my seat, throwing another glance at the window.

"They won't bother you in here," Gambol said. "Stop worrying."

"They?" What did he know?

He waved dismissively before lifting the teapot and giving it a quick swish, then, grabbing a tea strainer to catch the leaves, he deftly poured the thick, dark liquid into the clumsily thrown pottery beakers he favoured. He preferred his tea black, but as before, he accommo-dated my non-goblin tastebuds by bringing in milk and sugar to help lighten what would otherwise be a pecu-liarly bitter brew.

He obviously considered us safe in here.

"Thank you for allowing me to come in," I said, moving on to surer footing. "You saved my bacon."

"Nuh-yeh." He shrugged, handing over a beaker of tea to me. "You certainly find yourself in some scrapes."

"You don't know the half of it." I accepted the tea, staring down at my mobile, hoping it would suddenly burst into life. If Minsk had made it back to Wonderland—and I had everything crossed she had—she would have been able to alert the others. Surely they would want to know my whereabouts. They would try and track me down. Perhaps alert Monkton to my plight.

"I don't want to know the half of it or even a quarter of it. Not even an eighth. Or an ounce—"

"I get the picture." I hurriedly interrupted the curmudgeonly old tyrant before he found an even smaller measurement to prove how little he cared about my predicament. But speaking of ounces, that reminded me of the confectionery I'd bought at the newsagent's in Tetris Alley. I unzipped my handbag and rummaged around inside, locating the worms. "Would you like a sweet?"

I waited for him to say no, he didn't care for sugary things, but he didn't. His eyes grew round, like a little boy at Christmas. "May I?" he asked, so nicely and politely, I might have imagined he'd turned into an entirely different person.

"Of course." I opened the bag wider and shook them in his direction. "Take a couple."

His ugly little hand reached out, almost warily, and he carefully selected a pair of long sugary worms, one yellow and pink, one yellow and green. "Oooh!" His breath rushed out in happiness as he stared at them in wonder. Surely he'd seen such sweets before? He switched one into his other hand and held them up in front of his face, smiling gleefully, making them dance.

"Almost too good to eat," he said and lay them both down next to his beaker.

"Impossible," I said and stuffed a whole one into my

mouth. Well, it had been a while since I'd eaten. A quick chew and it was gone.

He stared at me, quite appalled.

"Help yourself," I suggested.

He didn't though. He merely picked up the first, reverently, and nibbled at the head. Very telling. No point starting on the tail when you need to incapacitate it first. Suck out the brains and all hope of sentience disappears. Goblins: true predators.

Given that he was now slightly more affable, I decided it might be a good time to broach our previous meeting. "I've a bone to pick with you," I told him.

"I'm sure you're very good at picking bones," Gambol replied, not taking his eyes off the worm in his hand. His alarmingly green tongue darted out to catch a stray speck of the sour sugar.

"The last time we met, you spun me a web of lies about rabbits!"

Now he did look at me. "Not all lies." He pouted.

"What was all that nonsense? Quite the yarn you were spinning!"

He eyed me carefully. "Kept you on your toes. You're surely not telling me there are no rabbits?" His eyes glinted. "That would be an untruth, DI Liddell. Why don't you share with me what you know about the white rabbit?"

I backed off, thinking quickly. Minsk had told me she had no knowledge of Wizard Gambol. I could therefore only surmise that he wasn't a member of the Dark Squad. Alternatively, what were the chances that he *was* a member, but it was above her paygrade to know about him? Was this a test? He was a peculiar fellow, and I was growing suspicious that there was more to him than at first met the eye.

Culpeper might know more about Gambol, but I had no way of speaking to him unless he chose to invite me back beyond the portal in Packhorse Close. Given the secrecy with which the Dark Squad chose to operate, that seemed unlikely to happen.

How thoroughly confusing.

But Gambol knew about Minsk, or at least the existence of *a* white rabbit. Of actual brown rabbits, I'd seen neither hide nor hair.

Hare?

But of course, Snitch had seen one. I had no idea what the truth of the matter was. For now, I decided to play it safe. "There's nothing to tell." I'd protect Minsk at all costs. I had no idea what this belligerent old wizard was playing at, and until I knew for certain he was trustworthy—and I couldn't see that ever being the case—I'd remain schtum.

He shrugged.

The floor bounced again, causing the tea in my beaker to shimmy. What *was* causing that?

Wizard Gambol, however, appeared entirely unperturbed. He supped happily at his tea and nibbled on his worm.

Given that he wasn't in a rush to tell me anything, I tried a different tack. "When did you move?" I asked.

"Move?" His brow wrinkled, the overhang so heavy, I almost lost sight of his eyes.

"House. When did you move house?" I clarified.

"I've never moved house. I was born in this house. I still sleep in the same bedroom I always have."

I rolled my head around on my neck and sighed. Honestly! This chap was impossible. Recalcitrant. Disagreeable. Contrary. It was like having a conversation with sticky toffee pudding. Except I liked sticky toffee pudding.

"When I first met you, you were in Packhorse Close. When I went back, you'd gone. I never quite understood that—how you managed to suddenly disappear—but here you are. You've upped and moved"—I gestured around at his furnishings—"lock, stock and barrel."

"Ah, yes." He nodded slowly. "To be fair, in that sense, I've moved."

I drained my tea. Despite the strong tang and overt bitterness, it had refreshed me. My brain began to feel a little more alert and some strength returned to my weary legs. Even so, Gambol's riddles were mentally exhausting. I needed to get back to the office and check in with everyone. If I couldn't get a mobile signal here, I'd have to risk heading back outside. Perhaps Wizard Gambol would be good enough to offer directions.

"Why are they after you?" The wizard had picked up his second worm. I could tell he was about to repeat the whole laborious process of dissecting it, millimetre by millimetre, all over again. I'd never known anyone take as long to eat a sweet as this guy.

"I assume they think I'm onto something, but from my point of view, I don't know what yet."

"This is the investigation into the dead wizard?" Gambol tilted his head to watch my expression.

"In part."

"I don't like the notion of dead wizards. We're a rare and distinguished breed."

This was Tumble Town. Wizards were hardly rare! And, most of the ones I'd met recently had been a rare and distinguished pain in the backside. "To be honest, I was following up a lead on a young woman who was murdered in Peachstone Market this morning."

"Who was that then?"

"I doubt whether you know her. She was a flower seller. Her name was Lily Rose Budd."

For the minutest moment, he became still and I sensed something shift in the room. He swiftly recovered himself, though, and continued to nibble on his worm head.

"Are you—" I fumbled for the words. "Did you know her?"

"No," he snapped, his expression closing down. "I didn't know her. I don't know anything about anyone."

That was a lie, pure and simple.

"Wizard Gambol—"

"I know nothing!" He stuffed the worm into his mouth, chewed viciously and swallowed it.

Placing my beaker on the tray, I stood. "If it's safe, I should make a move."

He didn't protest. Didn't even look at me.

"Thanks for allowing me to take shelter here," I repeated. "And for the tea." I had genuinely quite enjoyed it. "You couldn't point me back towards Tudor Lane or Cross Lane, could you, please?"

"I could," he said, and the light of mischief was back

in his eyes, "but if you can't find your way home from here, you shouldn't be out and about in Tumble Town at all!"

Impossible little mini-ogre!

Nodding, I picked up my bag and my mobile. "Fine. You can keep the bag of worms if you like," I said, maintaining my calm. I wouldn't let him know he was getting to me.

"Nuh-yeh!" He reached out and tapped the bag. "No, thank you." His tone was a tad more civilised now. "I couldn't possibly."

"Honest—"

"No."

"Okay." I reached for the paper bag, scrunched up the top and stuffed it back into my handbag. He hugged his beaker of tea and watched me leave the room, his lips pressed together. Alone in the hall, I pulled my boots on and leaned over to lace them up. Hoisting myself upright, I considered the magickal lock on the door. What waited for me outside? Who—

"There's no-one out there."

The wizard had moved to the living room door, his wand pulled out. He sounded fairly sure of himself. He beckoned with his left hand, and the green energy, fizzing around in the keyhole, unthreaded itself and reversed its trace towards his wand. There was a muted pop as the last of it abandoned its hiding place, then the sound of the lock turning.

Readying my own wand, I yanked the door open and stepped outside, half expecting to be confronted by two burly henchmen. Instead, I reeled in surprise. This wasn't the quiet cul-de-sac I'd entered less than thirty minutes previously; this was a busy thoroughfare. To my left, at the end of the lane, I could clearly see the bright lights of the shops on Celestial Street. Opposite me was a small, shuttered shop, ominously dark. On either side of Gambol's house were other equally small dwellings.

I was on Cross Lane, a long way from Tetris Alley and Northcross Street.

"How?"

I turned back to Wizard Gambol. He hadn't moved from his place at the end of the hallway, between the kitchen and the front room, still holding his wand out. The front door began to swing towards me.

"Wizard Gambol?" I called, but the door was closing relentlessly of its own accord.

"Farewell, DI Liddell," he said. "*Alibi locate!*"

The entire building shuddered as the door quietly closed. My vision shifted, or maybe it was the air around me—either way, when I blinked, I realised that the building, while not derelict, was empty.

I noted the number. Number 67 Cross Lane.

Curiouser and curiouser.

CHAPTER 9

"Where have you been?" Wootton scolded me as I walked through the door to the office. His face was pale, and his fringe was standing on end, as though he had been running his hands through it and pushing it back off his face. Bless him. He must have been worried.

And rightly so! "You wouldn't believe me if I told you." I swung behind my desk and dropped my bag on the chair.

"Do you mind?" Wizard Dodo protested.

"Oh, crikey." I'd forgotten all about him.

"Everything was nice and peaceful before you came back," he whined. "The phone hasn't rung for at least—"

The one on Ezra's desk started its familiar brrrrrrrurrrr, brurrrrr noise.

"Oh, never mind," Dodo grumbled.

I grabbed my bag and relocated to the spare desk, unzipped my jacket and threw it over the back of the cheap chair. Why did old narky-knickers get to sit on the most comfortable chair in the office?

"You smell … nice." Wootton wrinkled his nose "Bonfires and … something else. Have you been rolling in a smoking dung heap or something?"

"After a fashion." I plonked myself down and face-planted my forehead against the cool surface in front of me. I remained there for a few seconds, then, sighing deeply, sat upright once more. *Carry on, Detective Liddell.*

"There you are!" Minsk skipped out of the back office with a carrot between her paws, Hattie following closely behind. Hattie was quite taken with Minsk, although she couldn't quite get over the fact that Minsk wasn't the cute bunny-wunny she had first taken her for, but rather a hard-bitten Dark Squad detective. "I was beginning to get worried."

"We were considering calling in reinforcements," Ezra said, replacing the receiver. "That was Mickey. He's been trying to get hold of you."

I perked up at that. Was Mickey going to share some information with me? I reached for my phone.

Ezra held up a hand. "I wouldn't call him back yet. He was just on his way into another autopsy."

"Would you like a cuppa, Elise?" Hattie asked. "You look done in, my lovely!"

At least she wasn't offering *me* a carrot. Although I was so hungry, I would probably have eaten one. Plus, the bitter aftertaste of the goblin tea was so strong that maybe a carrot would have made a decent palette cleanser. "No thanks." I reached inside the top drawer of the desk instead. I kept a bottle of Blue Goblin hidden away—although everyone knew about it, so it wasn't a particularly good hiding place—and retrieved it now, just so I could unscrew the cap and sniff it.

I'd sworn off the beer the day after I'd become embroiled in the Dodo case, and now, while I wasn't seriously contemplating breaking the vow I'd made to myself, I was sorely tempted.

Wootton, still a little traumatised by what had happened to him after he had come searching for me previously, looked even more panicked. "What happened? Why have you been so long?"

"I—er—ufff!" I opened my mouth to explain, but simply made a kind of gasping noise that signified my confusion. "You know what? I have no idea." I pointed at Minsk, who had hopped up onto my desk. "One minute we were going our separate ways, the next I was being chased along Northcross Street ..." I trailed off and frowned. "Wootton, could you pass me a map of Tumble Town, please?"

He did so and I placed it flat on the desk, smoothing out the creases. When the ends kept curling up, I utilised both my bottle of vodka and Minsk as paperweights. If Minsk minded, she didn't say so. She tracked my finger, her whiskers tickling my skin as I traced backwards from Dead Man's Wharf to Tetris Alley, a small thin line on the map. Northcross Street crossed it less than halfway down. But when I traced the line that way, it appeared there had been some mistake. Northcross Street supposedly wasn't any longer than Tetris Alley and maybe half the length of Tudor Lane.

"Look at this," I said. "I was being chased. I ran. It

seemed as though I was running for a ridiculously long time. I was getting tired, but I shouldn't have been."

"Magick, for sure." Minsk's nose twitched as though she could smell trouble. "And not of the good kind."

"Someone was following me." I thought back to the sound of the footsteps. The tapping of shoes on cobbles. "Not one person but two."

Ezra raised his eyebrows. "Did you get a look at them?"

"No. Initially I thought it was the Viking, but now I'm not so sure."

"The Viking?" Ezra looked confused.

"The guy I met at Wasted Youth Tattoos when I was out searching for Wootton. Remember?"

"Yeah." He didn't sound so sure.

I relayed everything that had happened to me, from meeting Glossop, the market inspector, to the long chase into the cul-de-sac.

"Oh, Elise!" Hattie was beside herself. "You shouldn't take such risks!"

"I thought we'd had the Viking, as you call him, checked out," Minsk said. "We rounded up quite a few of the gang who were involved in Wootton's abduction."

Wootton mock shivered. "I'm still not sure it's safe to walk the streets yet."

Minsk tutted. "You can't let a couple of wrong'uns get you down." She peered up at me, gorgeous eyelashes framing those intelligent chocolate eyes of hers. "I'll ask Culpeper about him. See what he says."

"Good idea."

"And what happened then?" Hattie asked, hunching

her shoulders and squeezing her well-rouged cheeks between her hands. "I dread to ask."

I pulled a face. "Then it became even weirder. I banged on a door, and it just happened to be the home of a certain Wizard Glyrk Gambol."

"Who?" Hattie asked. "Do we know him?"

Ezra frowned. "The chap you met down Packhorse Close?"

"Bingo!" I jabbed my finger his way. "You win a prize. The one who spun me a line about rabbits, that turned out not to be quite the full story."

"Ahem," coughed Minsk.

I smiled down at her, resisting the urge to stroke her head. I knew she didn't like that. She wasn't a pet and didn't like to be treated as such. Unless it was Hattie doing the stroking. For some reason, Hattie was allowed to venture into rabbit caressing in a way the rest of us were not.

"What did he have to say for himself this time?" Ezra asked.

"It wasn't so much what he said as what he did." I shook my head. What I'd witnessed today had been some grand magick. "His house moved. It literally transplanted itself from the cul-de-sac to Cross Lane."

"The *whole* house?" Wootton sounded impressed. "Wow!"

"Yep. The whole house. The walls, the carpet, the kitchen, every photo, every piece of crockery. It moved in its entirety without a single thing being damaged. There was a little bit of shaking when the house settled"—that brought a whole new meaning to the word 'settled'—"and that was all."

"Interesting." Ezra plucked a pencil from his pen pot and scrawled on his notepad. "I'd like to take a look into him."

"You've had a busy day!" Hattie soothed me. "You'll be in need of an early night."

"You're not wrong."

"Let me make you that cup of tea." Hattie bustled towards the back office. "Then I'd better get back to my shop or my customer orders will be delayed."

Minsk offered me a bite of her carrot. The time she took to nibble on it reminded me of Wizard Gambol's approach to consuming sour worms. Stuff it in, that was my mantra. There was never sufficient time in the day for food.

Snitch picked that moment to appear out of nowhere. How he managed to slip up the stairs without anyone hearing him was always a mystery to me, but that's why he was so good at being a police informant I suppose. He had a definite knack for being clandestine.

"Alright, people?" he said, looking around uncertainly. I considered him one of the team nowadays, but I had a feeling he still felt like some kind of interloper, that he shouldn't walk among us for some strange reason.

"Alright, mate?" Wootton replied. "Hattie just put the kettle on if you fancy a cuppa."

"I'd love a cuppa!" Snitch enthused. "I haven't had me breakfast yet."

"It's after five," Wootton said. "It's going-home-to-dinner time." He glanced at me slyly.

We had no set work hours. I pretty much lived at the office unless I was running or sleeping, but obviously I didn't expect Wootton to do so. Nonetheless, he never minded about the long hours when we were investigating a case, or coming in at weekends from time to time. *Aye, aye*, I thought. Why was he in a rush to go home this evening?

"Hot date?" I asked, amused.

"As it happens ..." Wootton replied, then flushed and clammed up.

Hiding my glee at his bashfulness, I waved him away. "Of course. Be off with you!"

"Too kind!" Wootton grabbed his jacket and a number of papers from his desk. "This is what I have for you today. I'll go through everything with you in the morning, if that's alright with you."

"No problem." I took the mostly printed pages from him and cast a cursory glance over them. Nothing pressing. Just a bit of background research into a few of the cases we had on the boil at the moment.

He paused at the door. "Although, you know, if there's anything you need me to do—"

"Not at all—" I shook my head.

"Or if you don't understand anything—"

"Wootton!" I gave him a look. "Go."

"You can always give me a ring."

What? Was the boy mad? How to impress a future love interest. Take calls from your boss in the middle of a romantic supper.

"I will do," I lied. "Just go."

"It's just I know how much you rely on me to keep you organised, Grandma."

I arched an eyebrow. "Did you want to be working unpaid overtime for the rest of the week?"

"I'm gone!" He laughed and disappeared down the stairs.

"Call him when he's on a date?" I muttered. "The boy's gone crazy."

Speaking of crazy, that reminded me. "Snitch?"

He'd been hovering in the background, not sure where to put himself. Now he stood a little straighter.

"I need a burner phone. Maybe a couple."

" 'S not a problem, DC Liddell." He regarded me seriously. "I can get you a bundle from a chap I know—"

"He can't know they're for me," I cautioned.

Snitch tapped his nose. "Say no more. Loose tongues and all that."

"Exactly."

"I'll need cash up front, mind," Snitch said. "He won't give me nuffink on credit."

Of course, he wouldn't. The Tumble Town economy didn't work that way.

I mooched over to Wootton's desk and pulled open the bottom drawer where we kept the petty cash tin. Pulling out a bundle of notes, I waved them at Snitch. "How much will you need?"

Snitch slid over and stared—wide-eyed—at the amount of cash I held in my hand. "Ooooh." After a moment he licked his lips and reached towards the money, sliding a few notes out of the bunch with filthy fingertips. "I'll take a red one and a couple of purple ones."

"Ninety quid?" Ezra erupted, making Snitch jump. "What are you buying us? iPhones?"

"I shouldn't have thought so, DS Izax. Was it iPhones you wanted, though? They cost a bit more."

"Ignore him," I told Snitch, glaring at Ezra. "Any chance of a receipt?"

Snitch stared at me as though I'd grown a second head. "I'd say that was unlikely, DC Liddell. He don't like to keep a paper trail, my mate."

Ezra snorted. "I doubt whether any of Snitch's contacts can read or write anyway."

All good points.

Hattie returned with two mugs of tea. "Here we are. Tea for the workers."

Snitch glowed, probably made up to be referred to as a worker, and flashed his gap-toothed smile. "Thank you, Miss Dashery!" He waved the notes at me. "I'll be right back!"

"You can drink your tea first!" I called after him, but he'd already disappeared.

By the time he reappeared, his tea had gone cold.

He approached the door silently, as was his tendency, and it wasn't until he sniffed loudly to alert me to his presence that I realised he was there.

"Cripes, Snitch! You'll be the death of me!"

He emitted his snuffly laugh. "Beg your pardon, DC

Liddell." He held a filthy plastic supermarket bag aloft. "I managed to get you half a dozen. Hope that'll do you."

I reached for the bag. "That's more than ample, thank you."

"There's usually plenty more where they came from, just me mate has had a bit of a run on them of late. I brought some change back." He slipped me a twenty-pound note and cast a longing look at the mug of tea we'd left for him.

"Oh yeah?" That didn't sound good. Criminals used burner phones. If Tumble Town was rife with that kind of activity … it didn't bode well. Kept me busy, I suppose.

Emptying the bag on my desk, I sorted through them. Cheap and cheerful. Perfect. Snitch hovered close by, watching me.

"Do you mind if I drink me tea, DC Liddell?"

"I'll make you a fresh one if you want?" I offered.

"No need, no need! I wouldn't want to put you to any trouble." He picked up the mug. I could clearly see the film on top of the liquid. *Eurgh*!

"You're not drinking that!" I told him, clambering out of my seat. "Plug one of these phones into Wootton's charger over there while I make a fresh one."

"That's very kind of you, DC Liddell, but—"

"Just do as you're told."

"It's always wise to do what Elise tells you, my boy." Ezra nodded sagely. "Easier in the long run."

"What I want to know is why there's a woman in charge of my office?" Wizard Dodo squawked.

"It's not your office anymore," I reminded him. "Not your office, not your desk, not your chair."

"Whatever is the world coming to?" Dodo asked Ezra, ignoring me.

"All mine," I told him and wandered through into the back office, where I made myself busy in the kitchenette.

"No point asking me," I could hear Ezra saying. "I've never understood it either. Promoted way beyond her capabilities."

"Do you mind?" I shouted out to him. He laughed in response.

I shook my head. Ezra had never been an ambitious man. He'd started life as my superior when I'd first joined the murder squad, but I'd been promoted to his rank and then above him, in quick succession. He'd never minded, and we'd always had a fantastic working relationship.

By the time I'd finished making Snitch a fresh mug of tea and rejoined them in the main office, Dodo had fallen asleep again, his chin on his chest. Ezra was reading something on his computer screen and Snitch was sitting cross-legged on the floor next to Wootton's desk, surrounded by the phones.

He looked up as I approached. "It's nice to have Wizard Dodo around, isn't it? When he was killed, I was quite heartbroken, but now it's just like the old days."

Grunting, I handed his tea over. "It's great," I said, without much enthusiasm. "There'll be biscuits in Wootton's top drawer if you want to help yourself."

He didn't need telling twice. He reached up, pulled

the drawer open and extracted some Garibaldi biscuits. They had to be my least favourite in the whole world.

"Oooh, I love these," Snitch enthused.

"It's like eating dead flies," I muttered.

"Nowt wrong with that," Ezra said, without looking up. "Insects are a good source of protein."

"I'm not short of protein," I replied.

"I am," said Snitch, and stuffed a whole Garibaldi into his mouth. He chewed hard, once, twice, and swallowed, then held up one of the phones. "There's two with a little bit of charge on; I'll have to charge the others one at a time."

"I only need to make one quick phone call," I told him, reaching for the one in his hand. "The others can be stored until we need them."

What was that phone number again? A lot had happened since I'd spotted it in Glossop's office. I picked up a pen and scrawled what I could remember. Eight two—I remembered I'd thought it was nice and simple at the time—eight two three? Yes! That was it.

Thumbing the screen, I speed-dialled Tumble Town 823824. A moment of silence, followed by two rings, then a voicemail.

"Welcome to The Black Dahlia! Our opening hours are eight pm till four am, Wednesday to Saturday, and nine pm till two am on Sunday and Monday. We look forward to seeing you in our nightclub shortly."

"The Black Dahlia," I repeated, and hung up. "Anyone heard of that?"

"It's a nightclub," said Ezra. That much I knew.

"Over on Friar Gate," Snitch added, sweeping

crumbs from his chest. He'd demolished the whole packet of Garibaldis, I noted.

"Where's Friar Gate?" I asked.

"Over towards East Tumble Town." He had collected all the phones together into a neat pile.

I might have guessed. "Near Dead Man's Wharf?"

"Not that far north," Ezra said. "Near the old town's boundary."

"There was a monastery there once." Snitch could be a font of information sometimes.

That surprised me. "With proper Christian monks?"

"I don't think they were very Christian from what I've heard," Snitch said, but didn't elucidate.

"Why the sudden interest in The Black Dahlia?" Ezra asked.

"Because this morning's murder victim, Lily Rose Budd, left a phone number with the market inspector in lieu of her next of kin." I held up the burner phone. "I just called that number and wouldn't you know it, it's The Black Dahlia."

I nibbled on a thumbnail, pondering. "It might be worth paying them a visit, don't you think?"

"It can't hurt." Ezra yawned and stretched. "I'll come with you."

"No you won't." I folded my arms across my chest and leaned back in my chair. "It's a nightclub, Ezra. For *young* people."

"I think you might be guilty of pushing that definition yourself," Ezra returned.

"Maybe," I jibed, "but at least *I'm* not dead."

"I don't think they're that fussy," Snitch chipped in.

"About old people?" I clarified.

"About anyone." He shrugged. "It's a bit rough. You shouldn't go alone, DC Liddell."

"Oh." It was a shame Wootton had a date. I could have taken him along.

"I'd be pleased to escort you," Snitch said, flushing a little. "I mean, if you need company."

I weighed up the offer. Did I want to venture into a nightclub with Snitch? Not really. What about Ezra? Too old, too dead and too obviously a police officer. I considered calling Wootton and decided that would be unfair.

I'd either have to go alone—and today had already demonstrated why that was *not* a good idea—or take Snitch up on his kind offer.

Sighing, I slid the twenty-pound note he had returned to me earlier back across the desk in his direction. "Buy yourself a decent shirt and trousers," I told him. "I'll meet you outside The Pig and Pepper at nine."

CHAPTER 10

"**W**hat are you wearing?" I asked, aghast.

"Don't you like it?" Snitch slumped, hanging his head.

"Well—" What could I say to that? I had imagined when I gave him the twenty-pound note that he would have a mooch through Witchmark, a cheap and cheerful clothing shop at the Tumble Town end of Celestial Street, but evidently Snitch had thought differently. "It's original. I'll give you that."

That was the best I could come up with. He'd kitted himself out in lime green bell-bottoms, like something the seventies had tried desperately to forget, and mismatched those with a Hawaiian shirt in citrus yellow and flamingo pink. I would surely go blind this evening.

"I visited the vintage clothes shop on Copper Row. The lady in there has a bargain rail, and I thought these were quite zazzy."

"They are, indeed, quite zazzy." Whatever that meant.

"I brought you your change, DC Liddell." He held his hand out, wafting a crumpled tenner at me.

Ten pounds change from a twenty-pound note? He'd been robbed.

"Keep it. You can get the first round in," I said, wondering how to reconcile that with petty cash.

Snitch's eyes grew wide, and he fished an old wallet out of the back pocket of his bell-bottoms. Flipping it open, I could see it contained an old library card—more than likely, it wasn't even his—and not a lot else.

Poor Snitch.

He folded the ten pounds carefully into a hiding place and stuffed the wallet back into his trousers.

"Where did you get the platform boots from?" I asked. They were a cherry red with a three-inch sole, which made him almost as tall as me. "Were those from the vintage shop too?"

"No, no, DC Liddell—"

"Did he steal them?" a voice from a doorway asked.

Snitch glared into the dark corner. "No, I didn't—"

"Is he a thief?" asked a second voice.

"He's a thief!" cried a third.

"Stop thief!" called the first voice, and the call was taken up and began to echo around our vicinity.

"Stop thief!"

"Stop thief!"

"Will you give it a rest!" I growled. The Shadow People were complex. I hadn't managed to get my head around them yet. Sometimes they seemed to be on side, then the next time they'd dob you in to your enemy for the sheer amusement of it.

"I didn't steal them, DC Liddell. I borrowed them from a mate."

"Oh, he borrowed them," the first voice said, unable to hide its disappointment.

"Likely story," someone else threw out.

"Ssssh!" I hissed.

"They're a bit big for me, but I stuffed the toes with newspaper so my feet won't slip around so much."

I hid a smile. "Good thinking!"

Snitch preened for a second, before pulling a pair of mirrored sunglasses from the pocket of his shirt and slipping them on. I saw my face in them, recoiling in horror, and immediately rearranged my features.

"Let's get going, shall we?" I suggested, and Snitch, gesturing us down Tudor Lane, fell into step beside me.

"You look very lovely, DC Liddell," he said.

"Thank you!" I smiled. I'd made an effort, too, an effort to look like I hadn't made an effort, perhaps. I'd left work earlier than normal and headed back to my small flat, where I'd showered and washed my multi-coloured hair, then blow-dried it ruler straight, before pulling it back into a severe ponytail worn high on the back of the head—the way all the young pop stars currently seemed to like it—and primped my face with lots of make-up. As Ezra had pointed out, I was no spring chicken anymore, so maybe I wouldn't fool anyone about my age during the day, but under the cover of a few disco lights in a dark nightclub, I'd get away with it.

Surely?

Unlike Snitch raiding the rainbow chest of clothes, I'd chosen black. Short black leather skirt, old black t-shirt with capped sleeves, black tights and my long-suffering black Dr Martens. Elise's rules meant I always had to wear a pair of shoes that allowed me to run if I needed to. Early on in my career, I'd found that out the hard way. Tonight, I'd thrown on my trusty leather jacket too. It was handy to keep my wand, phone and purse in and saved carrying a bag.

"What are we hoping to find out when we get inside, DC Liddell?" Snitch asked.

"We're looking to find out if anyone knew Lily Rose Budd," I told him. "But we need to be subtle about it. We can't go in there and draw attention to ourselves because everyone will clam up."

"Alright."

"Maybe one way in would be to get into casual conversations and ask if they've heard about the murder in Peachstone Market this morning," I suggested.

"I can do that," Snitch announced. "I'm good at casual conversation."

I shot him a sideways look. I supposed he might be. That's how we'd met after all, when he'd started talking to me while I was propping up the bar in The Pig and Pepper on the night Dodo was killed.

"Just promise me you'll be subtle," I begged. "I've had enough trouble for one day."

"I promise."

It took us twenty minutes to walk to Friar Gate. The Black Dahlia turned out to be busier than I expected for a weekday evening. The building had been a factory once upon a time, in a row of similar structures. Several of these were now shut up and derelict, but The Black Dahlia was located in the basement of what looked a little like a packaging storage facility. Boxes were piled against the windows, preventing anyone from seeing inside.

Out here on the street, people of all ages were milling around. Carbon copies of me in my outfit—just much younger. Snitch, in his retro get-up, was going to stand out a mile.

So much for subtle.

Some of the revellers had evidently already been enjoying the local hospitality. One young woman, wearing a skirt so short it might have been a belt, was bending over to vomit into the gutter while her friend rubbed her back.

Nice.

I averted my eyes from all that nature had to show, and when Snitch didn't immediately look away, I elbowed him to get his attention. "Once we're inside, please don't call me DC Liddell," I reminded him.

"Ow alright, yeah," he agreed. "That would be a bit of a giveaway wouldn't it, DC—"

"Snitch!" I took a deep breath. "You'll have to call me Elise."

"Elise," he repeated, testing the word out. "Elise."

"That's right."

Taking his arm, I steered him towards the entrance. "At the first hint of trouble, get out. I'll meet you back at Wonderland if we get separated."

"Alright, DC—"

I raised a finger. "What did I say?"

"That's right. Sorry. I forgot already, didn't I? Elise. Elise. Elise." He drummed the side of his head with his knuckles, so hard I feared he would hurt himself.

"If I don't get back to Wonderland by—" I quickly considered my timings; it wasn't quite ten yet. I didn't want to be out all night. I was far too old for that. "Let's say by half twelve, you should ask Ezra to alert DCI Wyld."

"Will do!" Snitch chirruped.

We could hear the music now, a deep thumping bassline and electronic guitars. Fishing my purse out of my pocket, I said, "I'll pay and we'll crack on."

Snitch nodded and shadowed me to the door. "Elise, Elise, Elise," he muttered.

Two flights of stairs descended to the entrance of The Black Dahlia, which was deeper than I'd imagined from the outside. The club took up the whole of the basement. Once upon a time, it might have stored materials or goods—who knows—but there was still some evidence of industrial machinery around: substantial, odd-looking contraptions that would prove difficult to move, I imagined, and pulleys and ropes hanging from the ceiling. There was one enormous dance floor, the lights above it spinning at light speed with lasers shooting out in all directions. It was surrounded on three sides by open spaces, each with a bar, where the young and beautiful gathered to chat and to see and be seen. The fourth side was a mirror, giving the illusion that the already massive club was twice the size it actually was.

Quite intimidating in some ways.

Once inside, it was difficult to hear yourself think, let alone hold a conversation. It was one of those clubs where the music is so loud it almost has a physical presence. And it was packed too. People were gyrating around on the floor, hands in the air, whooping and hollering, and generally having a good time.

I followed Snitch to one of the bars—not an easy task because this one was five people deep—but he wormed his way through easily and pulled out his wallet with a flourish. You'd have thought he was a billionaire the way he was carrying on.

He leaned forward to shout in my ear. "What can I get you, DC—I mean—what would you like, *Elise*?"

I have to admit, I felt a moment of guilt. I didn't want him to spend that ten-pound note on me, but then I realised he genuinely wanted to buy me a drink—that he would be disappointed if I refused his kind offer—and so I pointed at the cola dispenser. "I'll just have a soft drink," I mouthed.

He nodded, his face serious. He knew I was on the wagon.

"But you have what you like," I yelled.

He opted for a pint of Hoodwinker, an old Tumble Town favourite, and handed over his tenner with relish. I noticed he didn't get much in the way of change. That was nightclubs all over.

We moved a little way from the bar and stood side by side, surveying the patrons. I'd been wrong to assume I'd be too old. There were people of a far more mature vintage than me here, although to be fair, most of those were men, probably on the lookout for younger women. And there were stacks of them to choose from, facsimiles of each other. I had never seen so many tattoos and piercings in one place, or so much flesh on show.

That's when you know you're past it, I suppose.

Snitch elbowed me and pointed. I followed his finger and spotted a tall, skinny fellow with long bleached hair hanging out at the edge of the dance floor. "I know him!" Snitch shouted. "I'll go and have a chat."

Nodding, I watched him join his friend, then retreated to a corner of the bar where I could people watch to my heart's content. The problem was the sheer number of people. Where could I start to find information about Lily in a place this crowded?

The issue resolved itself. For some reason, people— mostly men of a certain age but occasionally women too —gravitated towards me. Perhaps they were lonely and saw an opportunity to chat, certainly some of them were drunk, and a few of them even imagined I was in line for a romantic—or not so romantic—encounter. I engaged them in dialogue, found out a little about each one, dropped Lily into the conversation—how I was mourning the loss of a friend and did they know her?— and firmly rebuffed any advances. If I lay the grief on sufficiently heavily, it seemed to be an ideal way to send them packing. No-one who is after a fun time wants to hang out with a misery. Of course, one or two wanted to offer solace, but I rid myself of them by explaining I wanted to be alone.

Snitch and I touched base occasionally, usually when his drink had run out. I bought him a few beers and sent him away. For my part, I eked my cola drinks out, but after three of them, I found myself badly needing to pee.

The ladies toilets were the same as ladies toilets in every club I'd ever been in. The loo seats were missing, and there was little if any toilet roll on the holders—most of it being on the floor or around the sink areas because of course the air driers were all out of use and people who wanted to dry their hands used the loo roll.

I attended to business, thankful I had all my years of experience of nightclubs behind me and had remembered to stuff a couple of emergency tissues down my bra before leaving home, and exited my cubicle to wash my hands.

Women were coming in and out constantly, chatting loudly, all of them slightly deafened by the volume of music. Only one woman seemed out of place, just by her watchfulness, but even she fitted in physically. Dressed in a long top over fishnet tights, her hair streaked blue, she was leaning over a sink, staring into a mirror, her pale eyes oddly unfocused. When I joined her there, running the tap while trying to squeeze soap out of the blocked soap dispenser, she hurriedly pulled a lipstick out and began to apply the deep purple colour to her mouth.

When she checked me out, I nodded her way. "Hey," I said.

She returned my nod and pressed her lips together.

"It's a relief to be out of the noise," I said. "I'm not in the mood tonight."

Her reflection studied me. "You can always leave." Her voice was cool, deep. Taking a closer look, I realised her beautifully applied white pan make-up concealed her maturity. Her figure was that of a mere slip of a teenager, but the tiny lines around her eyes, cleverly masked by her concealer, suggested she might be older than me.

"You're right," I said. "I shouldn't have come here this evening."

She went back to studying her own face.

"I lost a friend today," I said, pretending to choke on my words. "I didn't want to be on my own, but—"

"I'm sorry to hear that." She returned her scrutiny, her voice still cool. I didn't sense a great deal of sympathy, and some instinct told me I'd wrong-footed myself. "Anybody I'd know?" she asked, wiping a tiny smudge of purple away from the corner of her mouth with the tip of her little finger.

"I don't know." Should I proceed or not? There was something about this stranger that didn't sit right with me, but I'd come here for info, and you didn't get apples unless you shook the tree. "Her name was Lily Rose Budd," I blurted.

She met my eyes in the mirror and froze for a fraction of a second. Then her lips curled slightly upwards at the corners, and she offered a minute lift of her shoulders. "Not a name I recognise." She clicked the lid of her lipstick back into place. "Sorry again," she said, and pivoted away.

I remained at the sink, watching in the mirror as she departed. As the door opened, the swell of music roared around the room, causing my head to pulse. She looked back once, caught my eye, then the door closed and she was lost from view. When I trailed her out a few seconds later, she had melted into the crowd.

I surveyed what I could see of the club. She mustn't have gone far, but I couldn't locate her. I'd lost track of Snitch too.

Reclaiming my place at the corner of the bar, like the wallflower I was, I found that the bartender had cleared my unfinished glass of cola away. Deciding to mix things up a little, I ordered a lemonade instead and was about to pay for it when a hand reached out and stopped me.

"My treat."

Turning, I found myself face to face with someone all too familiar. He'd spruced himself up for the evening, wearing leather trousers and a colourful silk shirt, and his hair had been freshly washed. It hung loose over his shoulders, the red catching the light. The Viking. I have to confess he was a handsome chap. He grinned at me and handed over a note to the bartender before I could prevent him from doing so. "Well, hell-oooo, darlin'. Fancy meeting you here."

I narrowed my eyes. "Yes, fancy. Are you following me?"

He affected an air of innocence. "Now why would I

do that?" He shook his head when the bartender offered him his change.

"Thank you, sir!" the bartender said.

Sir? I frowned. "I don't want you to buy my drinks."

"What you want and what you need are two very different things." He raised one eyebrow suggestively.

Exasperated, I turned away. When he reached out to catch my arm, I shook him off and glared at him. "You followed me this morning, didn't you?" I asked.

"I wanted to see what was so fascinating to you about Old Mother Mae's place."

"Not much as it turned out," I said.

"Uh-huh." His eyes were mesmerising. The pupils widened as they met mine.

"But you know that," I told him, "seeing as you came in after me."

A flicker of annoyance. He waved his hand, dismissing my comment. "What brings you to my club anyhow?"

"*Your* club?" That would explain the bartender calling him 'sir'. "I thought you were a tattooist."

"A man's gotta live," the Viking drawled, and winked at me.

"Fingers in many pies, eh?" I made a mental note of that. The more businesses he owned, the easier it would be for me to trace him and what he did.

"Something like that." He leaned closer to me, his long hair brushing against my hand. It sent a little shiver down my back. I thought of George Gilchrist, my sometime love, and pulled myself together, arching my head away from him, grabbing the bar to balance myself.

But he didn't give up. He nuzzled close. "A little birdie tells me you've been here asking after someone."

Oh, yes? "Did that little birdie have blue hair and white pan make-up by any chance?"

"Tell me who it is you're enquiring about." He placed his huge hand over mine. He could have crushed my fingers easily.

"I'm not going to do that," I told him. "It's none of your business."

"I think it is, *Detective*."

We stared at each other, faces so close that to any casual observer we might have appeared intimate. In a way, we were. There was something surprising in his expression, some quiet longing that spoke of vulnerability.

"Please," he said, and any edge had deserted his tone. "Tell me."

"Lily Rose Budd," I said. "She gave her next of kin as the number of the nightclub."

A low keening sound whistled out of him, and for a fraction of time, I saw real pain as his face twisted. "Next of kin?" he repeated, his voice flat.

"Yes." I could hardly hide my surprise. "Did you know her?"

"Did I know her?" That same tone. "You're telling me she's dead."

This was not the reaction I'd been expecting. "You did know her," I said. "She was one of yours?"

He flinched. "One of my what?" he snapped. "Henchmen? Hard jobs?"

"Whoa!" I stepped away from him and his sudden aggression, holding my hands up.

He pulled me back. "How did it happen?" He was making a huge effort to keep his tone casual.

"Someone attacked her on Peachstone Market."

"Attacked?"

"She was stabbed, I believe. Just the once."

He squeezed my wrist. "By whom?"

"I don't know."

"Did she suffer?"

"No. I think it was instantaneous."

He slammed a fist against the counter, and the bartender reeled away, spilling the pint he was pouring for another customer.

"What happened to her belongings?"

"Belongings?" I repeated stupidly. "All there was were flowers in baskets—"

"What happened to them?"

"The police took them," I lied.

He looked away, staring into the crowd of people on the dance floor.

"You have to tell me what you know about her," I said. "If she was one of yours—"

He recovered himself, glanced hurriedly around once more, then rubbed his face with one colossal paw. When he looked back at me, the swagger had returned.

"She wasn't one of mine. You need to leave."

"Wait a minute!"

He gestured towards a burly chap waiting by the

door. "Jojo?" he called. The heavyweight swung our way, the floor bouncing under his bulk as he charged towards me. I decided making myself scarce might be a good idea. I didn't want to feel the weight of Jojo's displeasure.

"Alright, Elise?" A quiet voice at my elbow.

Snitch had found me.

"Alright, Mr Lemsta?"

I stared at Snitch in surprise. "You know each other?"

"We've had a couple of dealings from time to time, haven't we, Mr Lemsta?" Snitch doffed an imaginary hat at the Viking. "Always available if you need any errands running, sir."

Jojo had joined us. He clasped his hands together and cracked his knuckles.

"We were just leaving," I told him, grabbing hold of Snitch's upper arm. "Come on!"

"Ow! Okay. Bye Mr Lemsta!"

I hustled Snitch up the stairs of the basement, past the reception, past the blue-haired woman leaning against the doorframe and smoking a cigarette, out of the club and into the cooler air outside. My ears were ringing, and sweat prickled my skin. Around us, drunken partygoers weaved this way and that, one or two of them arguing, one woman crying hysterically, another moaning about losing a shoe. I pulled Snitch away from the club, shuffling down Friar Gate a little way before glancing back.

The Viking, also known as Mr Lemsta, stood at the door beside the blue-haired woman, watching us.

My heart was beating at a heightened tempo. I expected to see malice in his expression, was preparing to have to make a run for it, but instead, I only saw moisture shining in his eyes.

Was he crying?

He caught me looking, blinked and stepped back into the nightclub—and away from my intrusive stare.

CHAPTER 11

Snitch kindly walked me home, although it didn't seem strictly necessary. Around us, the Shadow People whispered and snored, but even they didn't have a lot of energy at this time of the morning. Which is not to say that the cramped alleys and lanes of Tumble Town were deserted. Not by any means. There were plenty of residents attending to their business. There were those nocturnal creatures who slept by day and worked by night, and many witches and wizards who preferred the moonlight to the daylight. The unscrupulous and the highly secretive conducted their dark affairs out of the direct gaze of people like me, who might otherwise have taken a dim view of their undertakings.

Men and women in long cloaks, the hoods pulled low over their eyes, slipped in and out of doorways. One or two passed us, turning their backs as they sidled by, averting their faces from view. Occasionally one would whisper to us as they brushed by—

"Personalised death hex?"

"Illicit potions? You want?"

Treasure seekers, people smugglers, tarot readers, genuine psychics, goblin masseurs, goat herders—you name it, you could find it in Tumble Town between the hours of midnight and four in the morning.

We shrugged them off and moved doggedly on. I'd found that the best way to deal with these passers-by was to pretend not to notice them, just keep my face forward and my eyes unseeing.

It was with some relief that I sent Snitch on his way and locked my front door behind me. I took a few moments to douse my face with warm water and get the worst of the make-up off, and then run my toothbrush around my mouth before crashing face first into bed and passing out with exhaustion.

But my dreams were troubled.

I found myself running down long alleys, endless stretches of narrow cobbled streets with no exits in sight. Arms reached for me, claw-like hands pulling at my clothes, long nails scratching my face, hooked fingers tugging at my hair. Instead of lamps, the streets were lit by lasers, bouncing off disco balls, and every-where I turned I could see people glaring out of windows, blue-haired women whose thick make-up cracked and flaked revealing ancient green goblin wizards beneath, nibbling on worms, long green tongues flicking at stray pieces of sugar. Voices in the shadows shrieked and cackled.

Run.

Run.

RUN!

I woke with a yelp at dawn, and no amount of thumping the pillow or tossing and turning could help me find a comfy spot in my usually comfortable bed. Just after six I gave up, traipsed into the kitchen to put the kettle on and then drowned myself under a hot shower, enjoying the heaviness of the water as it pummelled my scalp and re-energised me.

Twenty-five minutes later, my hair wrapped in a towel and my body in my old snuggly towelling robe, I curled up in the big armchair by the window of my front room. As my hands wrapped around my favourite coffee mug, I blinked out into the daylight, watching as the market began to slowly come alive.

There was Glossop, wandering around the stalls, bidding the stallholders a good morning as they arrived to begin setting up for the day. The earliest starters tended to be those selling fresh vegetables, meat and fish, herbs and ointments and ingredients for potions and spells. Clothes, household items, familiars and wands turned up later but then stayed on to catch the evening crowd.

A twisted little witch, whose name I didn't know, flung the doors of her food trailer open. It was a tiny thing, not much bigger than a portaloo, but she served the most amazing food out of it. She'd called her business Small Fry and was popular on the market for her bacon or sausage butties, her fried egg sarnies and her burgers and hot dogs. I have to confess, the smell of onions cooking always made my stomach rumble when I returned from a run.

Finishing my coffee, I began to consider getting ready for my day when a familiar lone figure caught my eye. Tall and well built, his long hair caught back in a low ponytail, and dressed more soberly than I'd ever seen, there was no doubting the Viking. Or Mr Lemsta, as Snitch had called him.

He glanced around—although fortunately not up at my second-floor window—as though worried that people might recognise him. He approached the fountain, Lily's fountain, and I realised he was clutching a simple bouquet of flowers. He knelt by the steps, his lips moving, although from this distance and behind my glass, I obviously couldn't hear what he was saying. He carefully placed the flowers so that they balanced against the stone. Standing, he touched his heart, and without further ado strode rapidly out of the market square and disappeared down a side alley.

I couldn't get dressed fast enough. Throwing on a pair of jogging bottoms, an old t-shirt and a pair of trainers without any socks, I sped down the stairs to the front door of my building and, carefully checking Mr Lemsta hadn't decided to return, jogged over to the fountain. Kneeling, I examined the flowers. There was a note, but it didn't give much away.

RIP A, it said, and was signed *T x*.

A?

We'd assumed, correctly, that Lily wasn't the flower seller's real name, but what did the A stand for?

And what was Mr Lemsta's relationship to her?

I decided that I'd make finding out my mission for the day.

Ezra snorted when I walked through the door.

"Something funny?" I asked, dumping my bag on my —sorry, Dodo's—desk.

The wizard woke with a start and glared at me. "Not you again," he grumbled. "Find your own office! I'm going to complain to Hattie about this."

"You can't complain to her," I reminded him, "she's the one who let the office to me in the first place!"

He was having none of that. "I'm fairly sure I signed a contract for this place. Did you?"

I hadn't, as it happened. When I didn't immediately respond, Dodo waved his finger at me. "Ha! Got you there, didn't I? I'll be talking to my lawyer at the earliest. Just you wait and see if I don't."

Rolling my eyes, I picked up my bag and moved to the spare desk. Anything for a quiet life.

"Where's Wootton?" I asked Ezra, doing my best to zone out Wizard Dodo's cackles of glee.

"That's what's amusing me. You both look like death warmed up today!" He chuckled again as Wootton crept out of the back office. "Not that *I* ever get warm," he added. "But I don't get cold either, so that's a plus."

"Coffee?" Wootton asked, his voice husky. The poor boy looked decidedly green around the gills.

"You look terrible!" I told him.

"Thanks, Grandma," he responded. "So do you."

"Cheers." In my case, I could blame the lack of sleep after a particularly trying day. What was Wootton's excuse?

"We were drinking dragon chasers," he explained. "Not a good idea on a school night."

Sidestepping him so I could get into the kitchen and turn the kettle on, I heard Ezra ask, "What, by all that's green, are dragon chasers?"

"Who knows?" Wootton answered. "I only know my head is exploding and my stomach is on fire."

"Some sort of red peppercorn and coffee liqueur concoction," I called through to them. Of course I knew what it was. I'd propped a bar up—far too often. I was more surprised that Wootton didn't know. He'd been employed as a bartender when I first met him. But I suppose The Pig and Pepper, the pub a few doors down from us, wasn't renowned for cocktails and fancy drinks. Spit and sawdust and barrels of ale all the way for Charles Lynch, the landlord.

"Sounds disgusting," Ezra said.

"It seemed like a good idea at the time." Wootton stroked his forehead with one hand and his stomach with another. "Maybe I need to visit a potioner? Get something to settle my insides." He regarded me, hope in his eyes. "Unless either of you knows any spells that will work?"

Dodo's strident voice rang out. "The best cure for what ails you, my lad, is to get on with some work."

I hid a smile. "I'll make *you* a coffee. That will be a start. It works for me. See how you feel in a few hours. Do you know any good potioners?"

"There's a guy my grandparents always swore by," Wootton said, gratefully heading for his desk. "Dr Quicker. I could try him."

After brewing a pot of coffee and depositing Wootton's mug on his desk, I fired up my computer and pulled a notebook towards me. "So … where are we at?" I asked, which was my way of convening a team meeting.

"Have you found out who killed me yet?" Dodo asked, always the first point of order on any agenda.

"We know who killed you," I reminded him. Cerys Pritchard—still languishing in a secure hospital and yet to go to trial—had, to my mind at least, been proven guilty. And we knew she had most likely done so at the behest of someone, probably the Labyrinth Society. Not knowing for definite, however, was a constant bugbear for me.

"Oh, that's right." Dodo pouted. "Wicked woman." I couldn't be sure whether he was talking about me or Cerys, but I decided for the sake of my sanity I wouldn't question it.

Wootton massaged his temples and focused. "I drew a complete blank on Lily Rose Budd."

"Me too," Ezra admitted.

"I may have made some progress in that direction." I tapped my notepad. "I went to The Black Dahlia last night—"

"The nightclub?" Wootton's jaw dropped.

"Yes. Snitch and I—"

"You went with Snitch?" Wootton's eyebrows disappeared behind his quiff.

"I heard that." Snitch's soft voice drifted from the landing. We all jumped. He chuckled. "That gave you a right scare, didn't it? You lot didn't know I was here!"

"Snitch!" I glared at him.

"Sorry, DC Liddell." Contrite as always, he slipped through the door to join us. He hovered on the periphery until I gestured him into a seat. "We had a good time last night, didn't we?" he asked.

I forced a smile. If it's too loud, you're too old, right? "A truly … marvellous … time."

"You were saying?" Ezra prompted me.

"I had an interesting conversation with a gentleman of my acquaintance," I told him. "The Viking, as I've always thought of him. Snitch tells me he's called Some-body Lester."

"Lemsta," Snitch corrected me.

"The guy you met at the tattoo shop?" Ezra's fore-head creased. "And then again yesterday? The one who chased you?"

"That's the one." I twiddled with my pen. "He joined me at the bar last night after I'd been making enquiries about Lily. He claimed not to, but he definitely knew her in some capacity."

"So you think she was one of them?" Ezra asked. "And she was on the marketplace, to what—? Keep an eye on you?"

"Maybe. Maybe not," I mused.

"If not you, then who?"

"I have no idea." Frowning, I remembered the tears in Lemsta's eyes. The flowers he had laid at the foun-tain. There was something deep there. That wasn't the action of a man grieving for a member of his team. Had they been close friends? Lovers?

"He's a nice man, Mr Lemsta," Snitch piped up.

Ezra blinked in surprise.

"Yes," I smiled. "It turns out our Snitch here knows him because he's worked for him."

"Who doesn't Snitch know?" Wootton asked. Perhaps the coffee was having the desired effect. He was less green, just ghostly pale.

I pointed my pen at Wootton. "So that's today job. Find out everything we can about Mr Lemsta."

"How are we spelling that?" Wootton asked, grabbing a pencil.

I motioned at Snitch. He looked horrified. "I don't know!"

"You don't know how it's spelt?" Wootton asked.

"I don't know how anything is spelt. I don't do words and writing and stuff."

"Not at all?" Wootton couldn't believe his ears. "Didn't you go to school?"

Snitch's bottom lip wobbled. "Sometimes."

Deciding we shouldn't go there, I cleared my throat. "Wootton? Why don't you just try all the variations you can think of. It seems like he has a number of businesses in Tumble Town, so if a name keeps coming up, it's likely that he will be the one."

Turning to Ezra, I told him, "Plus, we were right. Lily Budd is a pseudonym. I think her name began with an A, but that's not a lot of help to us."

"What's our plan today, then?"

"Why don't you and I go and chat with people on the market again," I suggested, wondering about the possibility of brunch at Small Fry. "It won't take long, and then we can follow up on anything Wootton's unearthed."

"Rightio." Ezra reached for his trilby and plonked it on his head.

"What about me?" Snitch asked. He wasn't officially a member of the team, but he liked to help out.

I grabbed my bag and jumped up. "I need you to find out where Lily Rose Budd—or whatever her real name was—actually lived. It must have been somewhere in Tumble Town."

"Say no more, DC Liddell." Snitch tapped his nose. "I'm on it."

"And keep Wootton in coffee and biscuits," I suggested.

"Biscuits?" Snitch perked up. "Cor."

"I'm not sure there's any left." Wootton looked thoroughly woebegone. "I had some Garibaldis but they've all disappeared."

"Have they?" Snitch asked sheepishly.

"Yes," Wootton lamented. "Are biscuits good for a hangover?"

I was pretty sure they wouldn't be, but then again, anything edible would be better than no food at all. "Buy some more from petty cash if you need to," I said, "if there's any left!" With that, I headed for the stairs.

I'd worry about explaining a shortfall in petty cash receipts at some other time.

CHAPTER 12

I imagined Ezra and I would be out for an hour or so. My intention had been just to have a quick chat with a few of the stallholders to see if they knew what Lily Budd's real name might have been. I assumed not, otherwise someone would have mentioned something before, but there was no harm in trying.

We began our interviews at the stalls closest to the fountain—a cauldron seller and someone who carved wooden instruments and burned elaborate symbols and designs into the wood—but it soon became obvious that even Lily, as friendly as she'd been, had shared very little about herself or her life with anyone else.

Ezra joined me as I purchased a sausage butty from Small Fry. Finally, after residing in Peachstone Market for all these months, I was able to stuff my face with one of these famous breakfast rolls. The rumours were true. These were the best sausage cobs in all of London.

If not Britain, in fact.

"Mmmm," I groaned appreciatively.

"Is that your breakfast or your lunch?" Ezra asked, shaking his head as I dropped a dollop of tomato ketchup on the ground. The splodge was instantly licked up by a stray dog that I'd often seen hanging around the Small Fry wagon.

"Who knows," I said. "It may just be something in between those two meals. We'll have to see how the day pans out."

"I'm not jealous," Ezra said, and the dog looked up at him, its dusty, fuzzy eyebrows twitching. He recognised a lie when he heard one, too.

I gestured at the Small Fry wagon. "I was *working*. I took the opportunity to ask the proprietor about Lily, but she didn't know much about her either. Apparently, she would buy a roll and a cup of tea twice a week. They would have a chat, but never about anything personal."

"What sort of stuff?" Ezra asked.

"Same as we've heard before. The weather. How busy the market was. Or not. Where the customers come from. Popular products. The kids—"

Besides the stray dogs, Tumble Town, especially around the marketplaces, was renowned for packs of feral kids. I had no idea whether anyone had ever truly tried to get to grips with the problem, and I didn't know anything about the personal circumstances of the children but, as an ex-copper, I knew better than most that unruly children had a tendency to end up on the wrong side of the law unless someone—social services, the local education department, law enforcement, youth or community organisations—intervened somewhere along the line.

"Exactly the same as I've heard," Ezra said.

"Can any of this be relevant to why she was killed?" I took a final bite of my heavenly sausage cob and offered the knob end to the dusty dog, who politely took the meagre offering, chewed once and swallowed before moving right along to the next lucky diner.

"Seems unlikely." Ezra pulled a notebook out from his pocket and jotted a few things down with his worn stub of a pencil anyway. My heart twanged a little. For as long as I could remember, Ezra had been using that same pencil to make notes. The eraser on the top of it had long since worn down and he'd looped an elastic band around it instead. Many had been the time I'd offered him a brand-new pencil, but he'd declined them all. His had become so short that I'd anticipated the day he couldn't feasibly write with it anymore.

But then he'd been killed.

And now he'd be writing with that tiny stub for all eternity.

He looked up to see me watching him. "Why are you getting all misty-eyed?" he asked.

"Indigestion." I wiped my hands on the teeny paper napkin I'd been given along with the sausage butty, balled it up and chucked it into the nearest wastebin.

Sensing eyes upon me, I glanced to my right. It's amazing how your brain can perceive when someone is observing you. I'd read an article once about how humans developed this particular survival skill way,

way back, the same way all animals did. If a predator picks you out as his next meal, it pays to be taking heed.

Glossop, the market inspector, was staring at me. I smiled and raised a hand and he gave me a curt nod in response. It was only when he turned away that I realised he wasn't wearing his uniform or lanyard. Either he was having a day off, or it hadn't been him at all.

Abandoning Ezra, I tailed the man I'd assumed to be Glossop a little way. Without glancing back, he began to walk a little faster, then he dodged between a rug stall and a clothes stall and was lost behind billowing sails of fabric.

Strange.

Curious, I backtracked slightly and wandered across to Sugar Row. Given how tiny the manager's office was, I had to get pretty close before I could see inside. There was Glossop, sitting at his desk, head lowered, a phone to ear.

It hadn't been him I'd seen.

"Twins," Ezra remarked, hovering at my elbow.

"Or brothers, perhaps?" *Huh.* Odd. But what did it matter? We retreated before Glossop could spot us ogling him.

"So, what now?" Ezra wanted to know. "Another sausage sandwich, or are you opting for bacon this time?"

"I know you think this is all a waste of time—"

"*Somebody* knows something—" he said, shrugging. "It's just *finding* that somebody." Ezra was nothing if not dogged.

"Let's go and have a chat with Bert on the off chance he's overheard something," I suggested. "He's the most likely to actually talk to us."

"Ya think?" Ezra asked, but he tagged along, nevertheless.

We dodged among the stalls, getting busy now as mid-morning approached. There were more ordinary housewives around. I call them ordinary, but you never knew what lurked below the surface. The most obvious-seeming and innocuous middle-aged woman could be a demon in disguise. Or not in disguise. Not all demons are horned, after all.

At first, I thought we must have taken a wrong turning; the place where Bert's market stall should be lay abandoned. A number of heavy wooden planks were lying across the iron scaffolding, and worn, faded canvas flapped above my head, but there was no sign of Bert or his fruit and vegetables.

Retracing our steps, I scrutinised the general area. No. This was it. This was where you'd always find Bert. Day in and day out. So where was he?

"Excuse me?" I caught the attention of the herbalist on the stall next door, the scent of burning sage making my eyes water. She finished serving her customer, twisting a brown paper bag neatly and handing it over before turning to me.

"Alright, sweetheart?"

"I'm looking for Bert." I gestured at the empty stall next door to hers, just in case she'd been on another planet for the past the-goddess-only-knows-how-many years and wasn't aware what her neighbour was called.

"Ain't we all, darlin'. Everyone's asking for him. He's a no-show."

"Any idea why?" I asked.

"None. I ain't his keeper, y'know." She sniffed and turned to the next person in line. "Yes, darlin'? What can I get ya?"

"Have you ever known him not show up before?" Ezra swooshed through her stall, as only ghosts can.

She glared at him. "Only when his old man, Lozza, died. Then Bert closed the stall for a day."

It would have to be serious for him to consider not turning up then. Presumably, he ordered all his fruit and vegetables in advance from the wholesalers. He'd be losing money hand over fist. I met Ezra's eyes. My own sense of grim foreboding was mirrored there.

"Has anyone checked up on him?" I asked.

"How would I know? That would be the market inspector's job now, wouldn't it?" The herbalist began winding long strings of some sort of orange ivy loosely around her fist.

"You're not worried?" Ezra asked, his tone even. He knew how to talk to people without getting them riled up. Me? I was a work in progress on that score.

She paused, her face softening. "Yeah, now you come to mention it, I am. It *is* kinda out of character for him not to be 'ere, and he's a good man. Always sends customers my way if he can."

"Salt of the earth," Ezra agreed.

"Exactly." The woman finished winding her ivy and carefully inserted it into a bag.

"I think maybe we'll check on him," Ezra told her. "Make certain everything's okay. I'll pass on your best."

"That's kind of you," the herbalist said, putty in his hands. All I could do was stand back and admire his technique.

"Number 14, St Boniface Rise, was it?"

The herbalist, offering change to her customer, shook her head absent-mindedly. "What you on about? He lives on Willow Gardens. Don't know the number."

"Ah, that's right, that was it." Ezra winked at me. "Cheers, love."

"No problem, sweetheart. Have a good day, now."

Shaking my head at Ezra's coaxing technique, I led him away from the market.

Willow Gardens was not, as you might have been forgiven for assuming, a green and pleasant environment. Once upon a time there might have been some sort of green area in the centre of what now amounted to a square cul-de-sac, but that area had long been given over to a stables that, judging by the dusky fragrance emanating within a fifty-yard radius, housed every donkey, ass and mule working in Tumble Town.

Obviously, these poor creatures had to live somewhere, but it had never occurred to me they wouldn't have access to fields and grass, somewhere nice to rest their weary bones at the end of a long day. Instead, this was it. This overbuilt yard in the middle of a hodge-podge of tall narrow houses, not a willow tree in sight.

Willow Gardens, my backside.

We stood at the entrance to the cul-de-sac and gazed around. Which of these was Bert's house? There was no way of telling simply by examining the exteriors. Because what sort of house would a greengrocer live in? If I'd thought much about it, I'd have imagined he had a huge garden burgeoning with ripe marrows and cabbages, but of course primarily, Bert was a market seller. Market sellers in Tumble Town didn't earn much of an income and tended to buy their produce from cut-price wholesalers.

Rather than guess where he lived, I held my nose and enquired at the stables, where a young boy, absolutely covered in muck and wearing a flat cap, gazed at me with a look of outright suspicion before Ezra worked his magick again and the boy pointed at a house with a blue door.

"Top floor," he said.

So, Bert didn't even own the whole building.

We entered through the front door—it wasn't locked —to find ourselves in a wide hallway, a pram parked under the stairs and a table for people's mail. I flicked through the untidy pile and found a couple of circulars and a bill addressed to Mr B Gooden—Bert—indicating that he hadn't been downstairs this morning.

I flicked my gaze upwards, and Ezra began to float up the stairs. Solidly built, and tiled sometime in the past forty years, I found, when I began to follow him, that I could do so without making any noise. We paused on the first landing and listened. Somewhere, behind one of the two doors here, a television was playing a well-known Witchflix soap opera. We couldn't hear anyone moving around.

On the second floor a baby was crying. That had to be the owner of the pram. I heard someone shushing the child, and it calmed down a little. Maybe it was teething.

That left the top floor. Even up here, I could smell the stables. I wasn't sure this was somewhere I would have chosen to live. Being on his stall—surrounded by fresh fruit and vegetables with the herbs lady next to him—must have been a welcome relief for Bert.

I pulled out my wand, not prepared to leave anything to chance, and followed the curve of the steps to the final landing. We didn't need to know whether he lived on the left or the right but, as I mounted the final few steps, I realised the door to my left was ajar. I could see through the gap; a pile of fruit boxes had been stacked in the hallway.

"Bert?" I called, still expecting him to answer. "Are you there?"

I pushed the door a little wider with the tip of my wand. "Bert?"

No answer. Ezra and I exchanged glances. He curled his lip a touch, a brief look of pain passing over his face. I'd seen that look too many times in the past. He hated it when we stumbled across yet another tragedy.

But that didn't mean that's what we were looking at here.

Did it?

I ran my wand over the edge of the door, looking for signs that it had been forced. There was nothing to suggest that had been the case. No splintering of wood; the lock hadn't been broken. The safety chain hung whole and loose and free.

"Bert?" I called again, but this time even I didn't sound hopeful. Stepping carefully into the hall, I found myself holding my breath. Beside me, the oranges freshened the air with their zesty scent, but I recognised an undercurrent of something thick and metallic and corrupt.

Something that made you instantly forget the whiff of the donkeys in the centre of the street outside.

A stench I'd recognise anywhere.

Murder.

CHAPTER 13

Pursing my lips, my back and neck rigid with tension, I crept forwards and peeped through the first door off the hallway on my right: the living room, attractively decorated with fresh magnolia walls and an ugly seventies sideboard. The relatively new television had been mounted to the wall. It was on but the sound had been turned down. Ezra flitted past me and gave the room the once-over. He shook his head. Nothing there.

Moving on, the next door was on my left. The kitchen. Even as I edged my head around the doorway, I knew what I would find. The stillness of the air, the hush of the world ...

A body on the tiled floor. A woman. She was surrounded by flowers, some loose, some tied in small posies. They weren't fresh. These were Lily's flowers. The basket had been upended, perhaps thrown into its resting place, partially under the kitchen table. Taking another few steps inside the room, I knelt and felt for a pulse. There wasn't one, and she was cool to the touch.

She'd been dead for a while.

Beneath her, there was a rapidly congealing puddle of blood. I didn't turn her over. There was no point, and I'd only end up contaminating the scene more than I was already doing. Instead, I retreated to the door and, with Ezra following behind, walked along the hallway a little further.

The next door opened onto a poky bathroom. Everything spick and span. Fresh towels on the rail. Nothing unusual in there at all. That left the bedrooms at the far end of the hall. The one on the right was the master. A cursory peek inside confirmed what I already knew.

Bert was dead.

He lay sprawled on his side next to the bed, his eyes fixed and unseeing, one hand across his chest. A thin trickle of blood squeezed out from beneath his fingers, a little more pooling on the carpet, already sticky. No point in venturing any further inside.

Ezra scanned the room for me while I checked the final bedroom. This must have once belonged to Bert's kids, but now it was a spare room, sparsely furnished. Mrs Gooden must have used it for ironing because the ironing board was set up and piles of clothes were arranged on the unmade bed.

Clothes they would never wear again.

Retreating into the hallway, I sucked in a breath and reached for my phone. Finding bodies never became any easier. But putting the processes in place, getting the ball rolling on an investigation—that I was familiar with. It was as comfortable as my favourite pyjamas.

I dialled.

Monkton answered within three rings. "This had better be good news," he grumbled. It was his mantra. As long as I'd known him, he'd been grouchy whenever I—or anyone else on the murder squad, come to that— had called him. But he loved it. He loved being in the centre of all the mayhem. I could hear a swell of noise behind him. Other detectives answering phones and calling out to each other, officers chattering ...

I missed that.

"As if I'd ever phone you with good news," I replied. "We don't have that sort of relationship."

"Thank goodness. So, what's the latest bad news, then?"

"Murder," I told him. "Probably connected to the flower seller—"

"Are you on the marketplace? What's it called?" The level of noise behind him subsided. I could imagine he had held his hand up to notify everyone of an incoming shout.

"Peachstone Market? No. I'm in Flat 7 of 11 Willow Gardens."

"Flat 7, 11 Willow Gardens," Monkton relayed. Detectives would be grabbing their jackets now. "What have you got?" he asked.

"Two deceased. Bert Gooden and his wife. Market stall holders. No sign of a break-in at the flat, but—" I retraced my steps to the kitchen, staring down at the flowers scattered around. Some of them had been smashed against the floor, scattering petals and leaves around.

"Yes?" Monkton asked.

"It might be a reach, but I think perhaps the suspect was looking for something."

"We're on our way," Monkton said and broke the connection.

"Why do you think they were looking for something?" Ezra asked.

"They were angry when they didn't find it," I said, pointing at the crushed flowers.

Ezra didn't seem convinced. "They didn't look particularly hard. The rest of the flat is spotless."

I followed him into the living room. The television was tuned to a sports channel. There was a bottle of beer on a side table next to an armchair that had been angled in such a way that the person sitting there would get the best view of the action. A couple of cushions had been squashed on the chair. It looked cosy.

"Bert was sitting there," I said.

The other person, Bert's wife presumably, had been sprawled on the sofa. An empty mug sat on the floor next to a women's magazine. They'd both been lounging here enjoying the football or tennis or whatever had been on at the time, and for some reason they'd turned the volume down.

"They had a visitor," I said. "One of them answered the door, and the volume was turned down so they could talk to whomever that was."

"Someone they knew," Ezra suggested. "The security chain had been taken off the hook."

"If they ever used it," I argued. "Not everyone does." I was guilty of that far too often. "But you're right. You wouldn't turn down the volume unless you were expecting to have some sort of conversation. That again suggests they knew their visitor."

"The visitor gained entrance"—Ezra pivoted, studying the scene—"and Bert turned down the volume to have a chat. There's no mess in here, no indication of violence."

"Perhaps they went through to the kitchen. Or they were talking in the hall and then it all blows up and the visitor lashes out at Bert's wife." We backtracked towards the kitchen. On the draining board, several clean plates and a wok had been left to drip dry. "No." I reconsidered what I was seeing. Dinner was over. They had settled down for the evening. Yet Bert's wife was in here. Their visitor maybe asked for something, and—"

"And Mrs Gooden came in here to give it to them." Ezra nodded. "I'm guessing it wasn't a cup of sugar."

"Or there's a difference of opinion." I tried a different theory out. "Perhaps the basket gets knocked to the floor at the same time the visitor attacks Mrs Gooden." I gazed down the hall towards the bedroom. "What would Bert have done if his wife had been hurt?"

"He'd have tried to stop the intruder, I'd imagine," Ezra said.

"Unless he was frightened and wanted to get away."

"If the intruder was armed"—Ezra pointed at the door—"Bert couldn't pass him to get out of the flat, and there's no separate exit."

"I'd still have wanted to hurt that person." A sudden

thought occurred to me. "Or what if there was more than one of them? Maybe Bert thought he was outnumbered."

"Entirely feasible."

"So, he runs to the bedroom." We walked along the hall together and peered inside. I pointed at an object on the carpet, close to the bed. "That's his mobile phone."

"He was trapped in the flat, trying to call for help," Ezra said. "And the intruder silenced him, because—"

"Because …" I formulated the idea slowly. "Because Bert and his wife knew what the intruder, or the intruders, were looking for. And because they knew him—or her or them—they could have identified their visitor to the police. To us, perhaps."

"If we knew what they were looking for, then we'd know *who* we were looking for."

"But that would be too easy," I joked. Macabre humour.

Lost in thought, I moved back to the kitchen doorway and stared in. No obvious sign of a murder weapon here or in the bedroom, suggesting the perpetrator had taken it with them. Perhaps they'd come equipped, too, intending to silence their victims.

Or perhaps they'd found what they were looking for.

An image from the previous day came back to me. A small woman, tiny and birdlike with silver hair coiled tightly around her head, her hand slipping inside the basket of flowers Bert had on display. Gentle soul that he was, he'd been trying to raise money for Lily's next of kin. That was the kind of selfless man he was.

I'd assumed the woman had been trying to rob him.

But what if she'd actually been looking for something that Lily kept in her flower basket?

"Could an old woman have done this?" I asked, wondering aloud.

Ezra took my question at face value. "Why would Bert have been afraid of an old woman? I'm sure he could have handled himself."

True. Bert hadn't been young, but he was certainly fit from lugging boxes of heavy vegetables around all day. But who knew what lay beneath the faded visage of the meekest of little old ladies.

Certainly, the one I was thinking of had been ice cold.

"A minute ago, you were alive to the possibility that there were two culprits," Ezra was pointing out.

A shiver of—what? Excitement? Fear? Apprehension?—ran down my back.

Because there *had* been two old women, hadn't there?

Partners.

Working in tandem.

"You're looking pensive, Liddell," Mickey O'Mahoney said, nudging my elbow. Dressed head to toe in a plastic suit, he was carrying a deep toolbox that was only half the size of the bags under his eyes. He was late on the scene, preceded much earlier by his assistant, Ruby. I'd been told that having worked a long day and well into the night yesterday on Lily Rose Budd's autopsy, among others, he'd been attending a messy magicide incident somewhere else today.

He was a busy man.

"Huh?" I blinked at him. I'd been forced to retreat towards the stables, although still within the cordoned-off area. Ezra had remained on scene in the apartment but had faded to invisibility so that he could eavesdrop on what was being said up there. A crowd was gathering a few feet from me, locals curious about all the sudden activity.

Around the entrance to number 11 Willow Gardens, I could see Monkton and his immediate boss, Yvonne Ibeus with her boss, Grisham Farley. The top brass was evidently giving Monkton a dressing-down. I could tell by his posture. He stood ramrod straight, nodding and saying "yes, ma'am" and "no, sir" every five seconds. I wondered what they were giving him grief about.

"Sorry," I said. "I was lost in thought."

"Solving the crime, were you?" Mickey chuckled.

"I wish." My thoughts were as muddy as a Devon bog.

"I don't know why you bother. You should just leave it to Wyld and his team." He gestured at Monkton. "He gets paid to clear up this sort of mess. All this stress can't be good for you."

"I don't find it stressful," I replied. It was an automatic response, but an honest one. I'm not sure I found my work any more stressful than any other aspect of my life. On the whole, and perversely, I kind of enjoyed it.

Unlike Monkton, who was withering under the tongue-lashing he was receiving.

"But *you're* a private investigator now. Surely no-one's paying you for this?" Mickey asked.

He had a point. I shrugged. "No, they're not, but … for some reason I think it's linked to my first case. The murder of Wizard Dodo."

"Ah! That reminds me. I knew there was something." Mickey wiggled a finger at me. "I was trying to reach you yesterday—"

"We've tried ringing you back."

"Yes, sorry, I've been too busy to return your calls today."

"What did you need to talk to me about?" I perked up. Maybe he had something interesting for me.

"The cause of death for our Lily Budd. Turns out she was stabbed through the heart with a slim implement."

"Ah!" I nodded in satisfaction.

Mickey laughed. "I thought you might like that."

"Like a letter opener?" I asked, because that would make it the same as Wizard Dodo's murder and I would like it even more.

"Not a letter opener, I don't think. Not even a stiletto blade. This was something almost rod-like."

"Rod-like," I repeated. *What sort of a weapon would that be?*

"It was a cool and calm job if ever I saw one," Mickey added. "Purposeful. The murderer knew what they were doing."

"Dr O'Mahoney?" A fully kitted-out technician was calling Mickey from the door of 11 Willow Gardens.

Monkton glanced our way. His superiors were finished with him. He didn't look happy.

Mickey waved a hand at the technician, making a move towards the house. "But what I most wanted to mention was that she had been stabbed twice."

"So, he or she wanted to make sure the job was done," I acknowledged.

He nodded and put down his toolbox momentarily to make a crossing gesture with his index fingers. "From slightly different angles, like this."

I repeated the movement. "That would be odd, wouldn't it?"

"It wouldn't be unheard of for a perpetrator to stab in one direction and then move—" Mickey pretended to stab his toolbox, sidestepped twice and stabbed it again before leaning over to pick it up. "But in my experience, murderers don't tend to dance around. They do the deed and move on."

I narrowed my eyes. "Are you suggesting there were two attackers?"

"I'm not suggesting anything. I only perform autopsies and present the facts. It's your job to interpret them."

"Dr O'Mahoney?" The technician at the door called out again.

"Or it was," he said.

"It *is*," I replied. "Have you told Wyld all this?"

"Of course." Mickey winked at me. "But I know you and he are on the same team."

"Dr O'Mahoney?" The technician was getting tetchy.

"I'd best get on." He walked away from me.

"Thanks!" I called after him.

Two attackers?

That was beginning to become a theme.

"DC Liddell?" A loud whisper to the left of me. I surveyed the crowd of onlookers. It took me a moment before I spotted Snitch. How one man could hide in plain view the way he did was a mystery to me.

An admirable skill, when you thought about it.

"DC Liddell?"

Ducking under the tape, I joined him at the rear of the stables. The pong here was at its worst. Behind the flimsy wattle and daub wall construction with its corrugated iron roof, I could hear the tramping of hooves.

"What's up?" I asked. "I thought you'd be looking after Wootton and eating all my biscuits."

Snitch snuffle-laughed. "We did manage to put away a few packets. But then I went out for a bit."

"And?"

"I think I may have found out some interesting information."

"Go on?"

"I think I found out where the flower seller was living."

CHAPTER 14

Craning my head back, I stared up at the austere building in front of us. A mid-Victorian tenement that might once have been vaguely attractive until someone had had the bright idea of applying grey pebble-dash that robbed it of all its character. Located about five minutes' walk from Peachstone Market, it was in a grim part of Tumble Town. Lots of dwellings, narrow streets, little light, but nothing to relieve the monotony or provide any kind of charm. On our walk over here, we'd found decreasing numbers of shops and businesses. This was little more than a dormitory, with—as far as I could see—no real sense of community.

"People have to live somewhere," I mused aloud.

"Beg your pardon, DC Liddell?" Snitch asked. We'd abandoned Ezra at Willow Gardens because I didn't know how to get hold of him without alerting Monkton and his team to my partner's invisible presence. Not wanting to give him away, I'd left him to his own devices but called Wootton—who even sounded deathly pale over the phone, if such a thing was at all possible— and told him what I was doing and where I was going.

Snitch was skulking in the shadows. I'd needed to bring him along so he could show me the way.

"Nothing," I said. "Just thinking aloud." I pointed up. "I'm going to go in."

"Shall I come?" Snitch asked.

I had a feeling that if I said no, he'd come anyway, so I cut my losses and jerked my head towards the front door. "Come on, then. Quietly."

Quiet was Snitch's middle name.

There were half a dozen steps up to badly varnished double doors with brass fittings. I'd expected some level of security but there appeared to be none whatsoever. The doors opened easily, and there was no doorman in the foyer. Above our heads were two fluorescent lights; one wasn't lit up at all, the other flicked on and off as though it were communicating with some higher being using the vehicle of illuminated morse code.

With no lift in the building, we had no option but to hike up to the sixth floor. Reasonably fit, I still found it an arduous climb, but Snitch managed it easily. I rested on the fourth floor, noting the layout. There were six units on every floor, all huddled around one small landing. On this level, two of the front doors stood ajar so I poked my nose into the nearest one. Tiny. Run down. Empty, bar a couple of pigeons who fluttered away nervously when I made myself known.

By the time we reached Lily's front door, I was the one breathing heavily. Snitch patiently examined his fingernails while I caught my breath. While my heart rate returned to normal, I leaned the side of my head against the door and listened.

No sound from inside.

Not that that meant anything.

Reaching for my wand, I ran it along the top of the doorframe and then marked a grid around the door itself, locating a bog-standard lever mortice deadlock. The safety chain was off. There were bolts top and bottom, but they weren't thrown into place.

"Are we going to break in?" Snitch asked in his loud whisper.

"Well I don't have a key, so what choice do we have?" I whispered back.

Casting a swift glance behind me at the other closed doors, I tapped my wand once. "*Unlock.*"

We heard a click, loud in the silence of the landing. Grasping the handle, I turned it and pushed. It opened easily, and I ushered Snitch in, quickly following him and closing the door quietly behind us.

I didn't need to say anything. Snitch remained subdued, respecting the sanctity of the space. Poor Lily had left early the previous day, not knowing that she would never return home.

But was *this* home?

The front door opened directly onto an open-plan living room and kitchen, the largest space in the house, but measuring only eight feet by twelve at a guess. Here, there was a ratty old sofa, sunken in the middle and covered with one of the cheap throws you could buy on Peachstone Market, and a multicoloured rag rug, possibly from the same stall. An old gas fire had been installed in the grate, possibly as long ago as the late 1960s. It had since been disconnected, but Lily, or somebody, had botched a repair. There were no radiators, no other form of heating in the room.

A tall bookcase, much painted over the years and currently in the same yellowy-cream as the walls, was the only other item of interest in the room. The shelves were lined with paperbacks: popular literature, with the emphasis on women's fiction and thrillers.

The kitchen took up one corner and consisted of a couple of worktops, the sink, some overhead cupboards, an old gas cooker and a rickety fridge-freezer. But at least Lily had stamped her personality on this area. She must have been someone who loved to cook. She had a basket, similar to her flower baskets, chock-full of fresh fruit and vegetables. Peering inside her fridge, I found leftovers in plastic containers. Her cupboards were stocked with pulses and pasta, spices and flour. Posies of flowers in jam jars were dotted around the kitchen. Tea towels hung from handles. A mug and a small bowl were upturned on the draining board, along with a couple of spoons. Everything was in its place. Waiting for her to come home.

Wordlessly, I drifted through a connecting door. The bedroom and bathroom mirrored the living room and kitchen in terms of space. The bed was a mattress on the floor, neatly made and comfortable. The walls in here had recently been repainted in a sweet pink. There were more flowers, beginning to wilt, this time arranged in old food cans. I guessed Lily had kept the flowers she didn't manage to sell on the market and brought them home to enliven her surroundings.

In the tiny bathroom I found her toothbrush, some soap, a couple of towels and a few cosmetics and creams. The bath was squeezed into a small space, the panel painted the same colour as the walls, the hose for the hand shower coiled around the taps.

"She didn't have much, did she?" Snitch finally broke his silence.

"No." I pulled open the one cupboard the bedroom possessed. Half a dozen hangers, hung with robes and dresses. Underwear arranged on the shelves. A single pair of shoes. A rucksack. "It's almost as though she was just visiting," I mused. "I've stayed in cottages for a week and taken more belongings than this with me."

"You've stayed in cottages?" Snitch sounded thoroughly perplexed.

"On holiday."

"Oh. A holiday. Yeah." He sniffed. "I've never had one of them."

I wasn't quite sure what to say to that. The levels of poverty in Tumble Town could be breathtaking. Of course he'd never had a holiday. I felt both guilty for mentioning my own and sorry for him. I was saved from having to reply by my mobile trilling. Relieved, I fished it out of my pocket, expecting it to be Wootton or Ezra, but it turned out to be Minsk.

"Hey," I said. "How's it going?"

She didn't bother with any preamble. "A little bird tells me you've stumbled across another murder, Elise."

"Bert Gooden and his wife from the market," I told her. "Such a rotten shame."

"And?" she asked impatiently. We hadn't known each other that long, but she definitely had a nose for when I was onto something. That's what came of being a rabbit, I suppose.

"And, I think I may have a theory I could run by you." She would instinctively understand my reluctance to explain over the phone.

"Where are you now?" Minsk didn't like to waste time. "Are you at the office?"

"No. We found Lily Budd's address. I'm in"—I checked with Snitch—"the old Otter Matches building on Longdogs Lane. Flat number 37."

"I'll come and find you."

"You don't have to—" I began to say, but she'd already rung off. "Oh." I stared at the phone screen. I ought to call Monkton and let him know that we'd found where Lily Budd lived, but with Minsk on the way, perhaps I should wait.

She wouldn't be long.

Yeah. He could wait.

Finding myself with a little time to spare, I took another look at Lily's clothes.

"What shall we do now?" Snitch asked.

I made my mind up. Handing him the phone, I said, "I want you to take photos."

"Alright," said Snitch, turning it over in his hands. "What of?"

"Pretty much everything." I stepped towards the sofa. "I'm going to do a quick search, but I need to make sure everything goes back in exactly the same position. Plus, having the photos will be a good record of the flat. I doubt we'll regain entry after DCI Wyld and the team have been here." I pulled a pair of latex gloves out of the pocket of my jeans. "Follow me around and let me know when you've got some good shots so I can get started."

Snitch nodded, his face serious. "Rightio, DC Liddell."

For the next ten minutes, I conducted my own slightly rushed fingertip search, moving cushions and rugs, feeling along the hem of the curtains, riffling through the pages of the paperback books, sorting through the basket of fruit and vegetables, stirring the jar of flour. Snitch took his job seriously, carefully composing the photos of the fruit and vegetable basket, angling my phone to get the best light, as though he was Man Ray photographing still life ... until I nudged him and told him to get on with it, bringing him back to earth with a thump.

We were in the bedroom by the time Minsk arrived twenty minutes later, and the search had yielded nothing that could help us.

I smoothed the bedroom rug back into position and straightened the quilt while Snitch answered the door. Minsk joined me in the bedroom, her whiskers twitching as she took in her surroundings.

"Sparse," she said.

"As though she had no intention of living here permanently," I agreed, standing up and brushing the hair out of my eyes. I'd worked hard and efficiently. I was feeling warm.

"Hmmm. Or as though she had another home some-where else?"

I regarded her thoughtfully. "Are you sure she isn't one of yours?"

Minsk lifted her nose and sniffed the air. "One can never be sure of anything where the Dark Squad are concerned, but I did ask Culpeper if he knew the name, and he said he didn't. I showed him an image we had sent over from the morgue with the autopsy report, and he didn't appear to recognise her."

"I just keep coming back to the fact that she was killed in a markedly similar way to Dodo. Stabbed through the heart."

"There may be no connection at all, of course."

"I know, I know." I stretched, almost out of ideas. "Do you think Culpeper would be aware of *all* the detectives employed within the Dark Squad?" I persisted.

"I honestly have no idea, Elise, but he's certainly high up in the echelons of power. He knows *a lot*."

I sighed.

"If you genuinely believe that the same people behind Dodo's murder are guilty of hers, then you're assuming she was on the same side as us?" Minsk said.

I didn't have a clue what side Lily had been on. "I would never assume there are only two sides," I told Minsk.

"Touché."

Snitch's eyes were boggling out of his thin weasel-like face. He monitored the conversation between Minsk and me carefully, his head swivelling on his shoulders as though he were at a Wimblewitch tennis match. "Cor," he said. "The things you detectives have to think about. Life's complicated, ain't it?"

Reaching out, I took the phone from him. "I need to call this in. Wyld will be furious if I don't."

"Have we finished the search?" Snitch asked.

"As much as we can. I can't knock down the walls or take up the floorboards or—"

"Belay that call!" Minsk ordered.

"But—" Wyld could be grumpy at the best of times, and he wouldn't be pleased if he found out I'd done my own search before he arrived.

"While I'm here, I might as well be of assistance."

"I—"

"Just give me five minutes to have a scout around. Rabbits have good noses." Before I could say anything else she began hopping around the room, her whiskers twitching overtime, her ears waggling, her little tail bobbing about.

I folded my arms and watched her. Snitch followed her around—from a safe distance—jerking backwards whenever she glanced his way.

"I can't find anything in here," she said. "Where next?"

I pointed at the bathroom, and Snitch hurriedly opened the door. Minsk disappeared inside. "That's not a bathtub," I heard her say, "that's a washing up bowl. Even I wouldn't get clean in there."

Snitch snuffle-laughed, and when I caught his eye, smiled. "She's amazing."

Poor man. He was completely in awe of Minsk, bless him.

As though to further enhance his admiration, seconds later Minsk called out, "In here, Elise."

How had I missed something in the bathroom? It was a teeny-tiny space with hardly anything in there. I frowned at Snitch—not that it was his fault, but he was blocking my entry—until he stepped backwards, then folded myself into the tiny room. Minsk was pawing at the bath panel.

"This smells of Lily, quite strongly. Just here."

I dropped to my knees. There were a number of Phillips screws with shiny heads embedded in the wooden panel. How could I not have spotted new screws in an otherwise dated interior? Extracting my wand, I tapped each screw in turn. *"Loosen!"* I demanded, and each of them began to turn anti-clock-wise until eventually gravity caught hold and they fell to the floor. Minsk curled her paw around one end, I took the other, and together we eased the wooden panel free.

Illuminating the tip of my wand, I pressed myself against the floor and squinted underneath the bath itself. "I can't see anything."

"Let me." Minsk slid under the bath, around to the other side. I heard her sneeze. "Wachoo! Ooh, it's dusty!"

"Can you see anything?"

"Slip your wand in a little further—there! Yes!" I heard scuffling sounds. A solitary spider, the size of a fifty pence piece, scuttled towards me. I shot backwards.

"Erm, hello? Where's the light gone?" an annoyed Minsk called out.

"Sorry." I didn't want to admit I wasn't a fan of creepy crawlies.

"Ach!" She scratched and thumped around a bit more. "There is something here, but it's gaffer-taped to the side of the bath and I can't free it."

"Can you guide my hand?" I asked. "Maybe—"

Snitch dropped to his knees beside me. "Why don't you let me have a go, DC Liddell?"

"Are you sure?" I was dubious, but I shifted to one side so that he had plenty of space to lie down and reach in. "Would you like my wand?" I asked.

"No, thank you," Snitch replied, polite as always. "Sometimes it helps to feel your way—"

I decided not to ask what he meant by that and, aiming my wand as best I could to get a little light down there, watched as he wriggled into a comfortable position.

"There, that's it!" Minsk told him. "Can you reach it?"

"Ah, yes." He writhed around on the floor, rather like a snake, rounding his body and elongating his arm, then held stock-still while he concentrated.

"Nearly there!" Minsk sounded excited.

"Got it!" Snitch sounded triumphant. The next second, he was sliding out from beneath the bath, covered in dust and cobwebs and goodness knows what else. Minsk came after him, her normally pristine white fur covered in a fine black sheen.

"Mould," she announced when I wrinkled my nose. I

would have offered to help her brush it off, but I knew she wouldn't appreciate that and, in any case, she was far more interested in what Snitch had in his hand.

He handed it over to me.

"Well done," I said. "You're worth your weight in Garibaldi biscuits."

"Aw, thanks, DC Liddell." Snitch preened. "That means a lot to me."

Crouching next to Minsk, so she could see what we were dealing with, I turned the package—small and wrapped in a blue plastic bag—over in my hands before pulling the remains of the gaffer tape away from it and gently easing the contents out.

A passport. A wadge of twenty-pound notes. A couple of photos. A single key.

That was it.

Flipping the passport open, I flicked through to the rear page. Despite the serious expression and set of the jaw, there was no mistaking Lily Budd, with her long dark hair falling over her shoulders. Except, the name wasn't Lily Rose Budd at all. Just as we'd theorised.

"Annie Angel Mendoza," I read aloud.

"Plenty of stamps in the passport," Minsk remarked. "Looks genuine to me. She's travelled."

I glanced through the pages. "Slovenia. Russia. Columbia. Mexico. Thailand. Lucky woman!" I waved the passport at Minsk. "Would you be able to use this to get some background on her?" I asked.

"Absolutely. When you get back to Wonderland, scan the pages and send them through to me."

I nodded. "Will do."

"What are the photos of?" Snitch wanted to know.

I spread them out on the bathroom floor. An older couple, smiling. A recent shot of a woman who looked a lot like Annie, cradling a small child.

"A sister, maybe?" Minsk articulated my own thoughts.

"And her parents?" I tapped the photo of the couple. This one had been taken some time ago.

There was no mistaking the final image. Lily—or Annie as I now had to think of her—wrapped in a loving embrace with our very own Lemsta, also known as the Viking.

They'd been an item.

I couldn't help but feel sorry for him—no wonder he'd been upset—but also confused. Was Lily one of 'them'? The Labyrinthians?

"She'd hidden all this away," Snitch mused. "But apart from the money"—he reached for the bundle of notes—"I don't know why she'd bother."

He hastily withdrew his hand as I gave it a sharp slap.

"Looks like a secret stash to me. A quick getaway kit." Minsk tapped the photos. "She couldn't bear to part with these."

That made sense. "And the key?" I picked it up. "Is this to another house? The place where she actually properly lives?"

Snitch plucked the key from my hand and turned it over. It was small and gold, with a number engraved on the bow. One-one-four.

"That's not a front door key," he announced confidently, and handed it back with a flourish.

"No?" I queried. "What is it, then?"

"It's one of them left luggage keys for a station, DC Liddell."

"How do you know this stuff?" I asked, but Snitch snuffle-laughed and declined to answer.

Minsk, brushing down her fur, chortled. "Best if you don't ask by the sound of it."

Shuffling the photos together and slipping them back inside the blue bag, I narrowed my eyes at Snitch. "Okay, Mastermind. Which station are we talking about?"

He shrugged. "I don't know that, DC Liddell. They usually have a little plastic keyring on them."

"Oh." Not much use after all. "Finding the correct locker at the right railway station in London, that would be an undertaking. I'm not keen to do that."

"Let's hope it doesn't come to it." Minsk had finished grooming herself as best as possible. "Now, shall I take another quick look around the rest of the flat?"

She was off before I could reply, bouncing around here and there and sniffing the skirting boards. There was nothing else to be discovered though. At that point I phoned Monkton and was relieved when he didn't answer. I left a message on his voicemail, telling him we had Lily's real name and address and asking him to visit me at Wonderland. I hung up, and we vacated the tiny apartment. After carefully locking up—using magick once again to secure the property—we traipsed downstairs and out into the cool air.

"I'll be in touch," Minsk told me, and hopped away. She wasn't one for long farewells.

Snitch's stomach rumbled loudly in the quiet of the narrow street.

"Sorry, DC Liddell," he muttered.

"When was the last time you ate?" I asked. "And I mean, properly. Not just biscuits."

"Oooh, I dunno. Sunday maybe. I visited Granny Gan-Gan and she offered me a bowl of stew."

I had no idea who Granny Gan-Gan was, but Sunday? No wonder Snitch was so skinny!

"You've been a total star today, Snitch," I said. "I think I should treat you to a slap-up tea when we get back to Wonderland."

"There's no need, DC—"

I held up a finger to silence him. A slight movement in the shadows behind him had caught my attention. He froze.

We waited.

When he opened his mouth to say something else, I shook my head slightly and he clamped it closed again. My eyes flickered left and right, my senses scanning for the slightest hint of something not quite right.

Nothing.

I relaxed. A little.

Behind me, a gas lamp sputtered, causing the shadows to temporarily lengthen. Perhaps that was all it had been.

Perhaps.

"Let's go," I told Snitch, keeping my voice low.

He nodded and fell into step beside me as we hurried away from the Otter Matches building.

As we came level with the doorway where I'd imagined I'd seen movement, I realised a pair of rats were cowering in the gloom. They glared out at me as I moved past, bright eyes glinting. I felt their scrutiny down the rest of Longdogs Lane.

In fact, I didn't shake the feeling we were being watched all the way back to Tudor Lane.

CHAPTER 15

"**D**id you find out who killed me yet?" Wizard Dodo hadn't moved on. It was good to come back to the office and find out nothing had changed.

Kind of.

"Wizard Dodo," Snitch jumped in before I could say anything, his voice patient. He evidently cared for the cranky old codger. "DC Liddell has told you who killed you. She's investigating who was behind it all."

Wootton arched an eyebrow at me. A little colour had returned to his cheeks, although he still looked a bit peaky. I must admit, a lack of sleep was catching up with me, too. My bones were aching and my energy was starting to drop. "Snitch is chipper," Wootton remarked. "What have you two been up to?"

"I'm glad you asked," I told him. "We've found out Lily Rose Budd's real name."

"Great!" Wootton pulled his notepad towards himself. "Fire away."

"I can do better than that." I handed the passport and photos over to my office assistant. "Can you make copies of these, please? One lot to be disseminated among ourselves, the other to be sent to Minsk."

"Rightio." He pushed back his chair.

"Do it fast. I'll have to hand these over to DCI Wyld, and there's a chance he'll be on my case sooner rather than later."

"No problem."

I examined the blue plastic bag in my hand. Only the money remained inside it, an elastic band looped around the bundle. How much was there? Easily a thousand, maybe two or three. "Better lock this in the safe for me as well, please."

He nodded.

"What does DC stand for anyway?" Dodo asked Snitch. "Don't care? Disinterested copper? Dilatory civilian?"

"More like dire cynic, like your good self," I muttered.

"What did you say?" Wizard Dodo bellowed, and, when I didn't answer, turned to Snitch. "What did she say?"

"She said she's doing all she can, Wizard Dodo. Dodo, chill, she said."

"Mmmm." Wizard Dodo didn't sound convinced. "In my day women weren't police officers, you know, and there were very good reasons for that."

"That's total claptrap." I couldn't help but respond. "There have been female police officers serving in one capacity or another for well over a hundred years—"

"Ah yes, but not with any authority," Dodo goaded. "And not useful in any practical sense."

"For goodness sake!" I found myself wishing I was the sort of witch who could cast hexes, maybe one that would send Dodo on to a better place. He was saved from my ire when my phone rang. "Liddell!" I barked into the receiver, sounding more like Ezra than I cared to admit.

"Who's pushing your buttons, Elise?" Minsk asked, her voice soft and smooth and calm. "You can't have been back long."

"I haven't." I glared at Dodo from underneath my fringe. "Everything alright?"

"Yes. I have some interesting intel to share."

"About Annie?"

"Indeed. Oh, wait." Her voice drifted away from the phone, then came back again. "I'm just getting your scans. Thanks for those."

Wootton returned from the rear office and dropped the originals on my desk before settling back into his own place and rapidly typing something.

I pulled the passport over and flicked through it once more, studying the face of Lily Budd as I had known her. She was older than I'd imagined. About my age, and yet she had carried off the deceit of being younger through her clothes and the way she acted. "What did you find out?" I asked.

"Special Branch."

"Excuse me?"

"I gave her details to our research team, and they

drew a blank. None of them had a high enough clearance. So I went to Culpeper instead. He made a phone call and confirmed we'd get nothing. She was MOW Special Branch, and that's the end of the matter."

I stared down at the photo of Annie and Lemsta together. What did that mean? Was she fraternising with the enemy? I'd heard of agents going deep undercover to infiltrate criminal gangs. Is that what had happened here?

"Meaning what exactly?" I asked. "What did she do?"

"Culpeper wasn't about to tell me—assuming he knows anything himself—but my understanding of MOWSB is that they collate intelligence and research into major organisations who pose a threat to national security, be that mundane or magickal."

That confirmed what little I knew about them. "And Culpeper can't find out what she was working on?"

"I'm going to push him on that, given we're assuming a link between whatever she was doing and the Labyrinthians." She paused. "That is what you're thinking, isn't it?"

"It is," I confirmed. "It's a mess. Too many players involved. Us. You. Special Branch. And no co-ordination."

"*We're* co-ordinating, aren't we?" Minsk enquired, and I could imagine her pink nose twitching and her soft brown eyes shining. "You and I?"

"Yes." That was something at least. "I'll see what I can find out from our end, and we'll catch up shortly."

"Good. Laterz!" Minsk broke the connection.

Snitch had succeeded in quietening Wizard Dodo down, for which I was mighty grateful. In the ensuing silence after I'd replaced the receiver in its cradle, Snitch's stomach gurgled again.

"Is it dinnertime?" Wootton asked.

"Sorry about that," Snitch said, casting a shy glance my way, reminding me that I had promised to treat him to something for dinner. I'd intended to take him to the pub for pie and mash, but given that realistically we were likely to be holed up in the office for a good few hours yet, it seemed some sort of takeaway was the answer. Reaching under my desk, I drew out my handbag and extracted my purse.

"Maybe I'll go and grab something for us to eat," I said. "What would people prefer?"

"Pizza," said Wootton automatically.

"Burgers," said Snitch.

"What about something a bit more grown-up?" I asked. "Thai? Indian? Ch—"

"Chinese!" Wootton and Snitch chorused in unison.

Smirking a little, pleased to have escaped the carbo-hydrate hell of pizza at least, I nodded and donned my jacket once more. "Back in a minute. Keep searching, Wootton. You need to earn your dinner."

"Sing for your supper, laddie," sniped Wizard Dodo. "That's what she wants you to do."

I made my way downstairs and checked in on Hattie. She declined my offer of sharing our feast on the grounds she had two clients dropping by and would be busy all evening. After promising to catch up with her later, I took off down Tudor Lane in the gloomy dusk in search of the Chinese restaurant and takeaway I'd spotted several times.

Yin and Yummy was located off a little side street. Its bright lights glowed with welcome warmth. Just the slightest whiff of soy sauce and my stomach contracted painfully. It had been a while since brunch, I supposed. I hovered in front of the menu taped to the inside of the glass. I should have asked everyone what their preference would be, but knowing them, they would eat anything and everything. I decided on a variety of meat, rice and noodle dishes, including a couple of vegetable ones in case Monkton decided to show up. Once inside and at the counter, I repeated my order, threw in a few bags of prawn crackers—mainly because for some reason I liked to eat them the day after, when they were slightly stale—and half a dozen cans of pop.

Chinese food always makes me thirsty.

Once I'd paid, I retreated to the seat in the window to read a two-day-old copy of *The Celestine Times*. The usual sort of thing. A witch caught stealing someone else's familiar. A number of break-ins reported at the off-licence near Herod's. Massive broomstick clearance at Witchland Discount Store.

More interesting were the births, deaths and marriages classifieds. I always enjoyed reading those for some reason. Especially the deaths. I was ghoulish that way.

Except this time, I was drawn to the births. Specifically to the birth of twins. Igor and Ilka, born to Petrova

Meadanski and her partner, Bob 'the sage' Smits. There was a small image of the babies, both dressed in an abundance of frothy lace, the little girl only distinguishable from her brother thanks to the enormous bow wrapped around her bald scalp.

Cute, I cooed inwardly. That's a handful, having twins.

Twins.

Everywhere.

The notion niggled at me. Twins and pairs of things. The old women. Glossop and his doppelgänger. Maybe his brother? The two unseen people following me after I ran away from Lemsta, so in tune with each other.

"Lady?"

The boy on the counter was holding up two white plastic sacks. My order.

"That was quick!" I jumped up, dropped the paper and took my feast from him. "Thank you."

Back outside, I hastened towards Tudor Lane and The Hat and Dashery, mainly because I didn't want the food to get cold, but also because thoughts were whirring around my head. Perhaps I was a little neurotic, but everywhere I looked I started to see pairs of things.

Two cats standing off against each other.

Two identical doorways, right down to the positioning of the letter box and the colour of the paint.

Two streetlights opposite each other. Neither of them working.

Two men, both with walking canes and top hats. Their faces turned away from mine.

Two donkeys clip-clopping away from me ... their little tails twitching solemnly.

The sheer ordinariness unnerved me, and I hastened onwards.

Arriving back at Wonderland, I practically ran up the stairs and burst into the office. Snitch was once again mollifying Dodo, who was complaining vociferously about nothing in particular, and Wootton was massaging his temples and beginning to look a little green again. Ezra had returned from Willow Gardens and had his feet up on his desk, his trilby pulled down over his face, striving to ignore the cacophony of Dodo and a pair of trilling phones.

I breathed a sigh of relief.

It felt like coming home.

Wootton and Snitch fell upon the takeaway like a pair of hungry wolves. By the time I'd found myself a fork—I had never learned how to use chopsticks properly, and it seemed a complete waste of time and energy to me to try to learn while my food slithered around and dropped in my lap before going cold, when a fork could solve the problem admirably—they had finished off the duck dish and started on the kung pao chicken as well as making inroads into both the chicken chow mein and the prawn chop suey. I hastily grabbed a bag of prawn crackers, the special fried rice and a can of sparkling orange pop and retreated behind my desk.

"This is totally nommy!" Wootton announced.

"Yum!" Snitch agreed, mouth full.

"I knew a Chinese wizard once," Wizard Dodo told us. "He didn't like rice. He lived on beansprouts. Faded away to nothing in the end."

"That's sad." Snitch, at least, was taking an interest in Dodo's bizarre stories.

"Yes." Dodo gestured around at the walls where his cluttered bookshelves had once stood. "I had some of his books here before you lot came."

I tugged at the ring pull on my can, listening to the satisfying hiss as the gas escaped.

"He was a wonderful spellcaster. Knew some especially intriguing hexes." Dodo was in a talkative mood. At least he was calm. That made for more pleasant company.

"Ooh!" Wootton had been swinging back on his chair, one eye on his computer screen. Now he jerked forward, slurping noodles hurriedly into his mouth before abandoning his carton to the side of his desk. "I've got mail!"

"From your girlfriend?" Ezra asked without moving.

"Nah." Wootton huffed. "I haven't heard from her today."

"If your hangover is anything to go by, maybe she isn't even up yet," I suggested. I remembered those days. Feeling like death after a surfeit of Blue Goblin.

"Meh." Wootton shook his head, pretending not to care. "No. I requested a search on one Annie Angel Mendoza on a database I sometimes use, and this contains the results."

"What have you got?" Now I was interested.

"Annie Mendoza, born on the fourteenth of July to Mark Gabriel Mendoza and his wife Angel Fortune Mendoza, née Ashbark. Mark Mendoza was a teacher of transmutation at Ravenswood, and his wife Angel was a witch and a member of the Coven of Truthsayers. Now both deceased."

"Oh." That must have been hard on Annie. No wonder she kept their photo in her getaway pack. It was all she had left. "How did they die?"

"Hmmm." Wootton scanned the information on his screen. "No data."

"Any siblings?"

"A sister. Older by two years. Gabriella Fortune Mendoza. Divorced. One son. Lives in Loughborough."

"Loughborough." I flicked through the photos we'd found. Annie with another woman. That had to be Gabriella. If Annie had kept the image with that of her parents, to me that suggested they were close. "See what you can find out about the sister." I took another mouthful of fried rice. "And you'd better pass that info on to DCI Wyld too. I'm sure his team will get to it, but it might take a while."

Ezra snorted from beneath his trilby.

"And they need to inform Annie's next of kin."

I sat back, chomping on a prawn cracker. Did I need to speak to Gabriella? What would she know? It might be worth a call.

The key we'd rescued from Annie's flat glinted on my desk, and I reached out with greasy fingers to touch it. The chances were that as a member of MOW Special Branch, Annie would have tried to keep her sister out of the loop wherever possible. She wouldn't have wanted her to be drawn into anything that might have jeopardised the safety of her or the child. Yes, I might have a chat with Gabriella, but I wouldn't expect our discussion to yield much in the way of useful information.

But assuming Annie occasionally visited her sister, would she take the train?

If I'd wanted to hide something, I would choose a place where it would not have been out of the ordinary for me to be, but somewhere busy and secure.

"Which station would you catch a train to Loughborough from?" I asked Wootton.

"You planning on taking a trip to see Gabriella?" he asked.

But Snitch had perked up like a little meerkat. He knew what I was thinking. "St Pancras, I believe, DC Liddell."

I abandoned my fried rice and grabbed my jacket. "Come on, Snitch."

"You can't seriously be up for travelling to Loughborough now, boss?" Wootton looked puzzled.

"We're not going to Loughborough," I told him. "Only St Pancras."

"I haven't finished me dinner!" Snitch complained.

"We'll heat it up when we get back," I promised.

"Owwwwwww." Snitch didn't sound happy.

"You're not supposed to re—" Wootton began, and I wagged my finger at him to shut him up.

"Sorry, Snitch. I'll make it up to you, I promise," I

commiserated and grabbed the key from my desk. "Let's go."

"I thought it must be too good to be true," Snitch muttered, pouting, but nonetheless he pushed his carton of bang bang pork to one side and pursued me out of the office.

CHAPTER 16

London St Pancras International was far busier than I'd expected. In my mind, people in the real world finished work between five and six, and commuters had scurried away from the city by half past six.

Not so.

This beautiful old railway station, originally constructed in the 1860s, was rammed with people heading north or rushing around looking for the Euro-tunnel terminus or the entrance to the London Underground. There were people pushing enormous suitcases on trolleys, others doing last-minute shopping. Many were eating and drinking in the cafes, restaurants and pubs, while a number of cleaners pushed brooms around, moving piles of dust, empty wrappers and food cartons from one area to the next. Burly security guards ambled here and there, heads pivoting as they gave everyone the evil eye. A pair of them closed in on some poor long-haired busker, gamely strumming his guitar even though he could barely be heard over the sound of the tannoy and the electronic announcement service.

"The train now standing on platform six is the slightly delayed service to Leeds. Calling at—"

Snitch and I stood in the middle of the melee, blinking under the bright lights and scanning our surroundings.

"Where now?" I asked. "Any ideas?"

Snitch, hunched up in his robes, stood out like a sore thumb here among the—mostly—mundane folk. He didn't like it one little bit. This was well outside his comfort zone, and I could tell he wanted to slink away somewhere no-one could see him.

The problem was that St Pancras, like most public spaces these days, was too well lit. There was nowhere for him to hide.

"Ideas?" Snitch asked, sounding a little sullen. I don't think he'd forgiven me yet for dragging him away from his supper.

"Yes. Where will we find the locker?"

"I don't know, DC Liddell. I've never been to this station before. I thought it would be obvious when we got here." The electronic voice announced a train to Edinburgh on platform eight, and there was a surge as people hastened to the gate. They jostled around us. "Oi!" Snitch called out after some particularly aggressive businessman in a dark, expensive suit nearly mowed us down.

"Alright." I tried to remain patient. "When you visit other railway stations, where are the lockers?"

"It varies." Snitch pointed up at some signs. "What do they say? Left luggage?"

I scanned the signs above my head. *Toilets. Underground. Information. Ticket Hall.* Yes! There! *Left Luggage.*

I grabbed Snitch's arm and pulled him after me. We fought against the tide of commuters, hard-wired to get home and take no prisoners in the process of doing so. We struggled towards the central part of the station as everyone else rammed into us from the side. Unfortunately, 'left luggage' in this instance meant a gigantic storeroom—rather like a cloakroom—operated by a female security guard who, at this time of the evening, appeared thoroughly irritable and put-upon. I joined the queue and was promptly disheartened. Everyone in front of me had some sort of app on their phone that they were using to reclaim their luggage and belongings.

When it was my turn, I held out the key.

"What's that, love?" she asked, her face blank.

"It's the key for my locker," I told her, affecting indifference.

"Which locker might that be?" Her tone was neutral, but her body language was combative. I had a feeling she would happily bite my head clear off my shoulders given half a chance.

"Erm, number one hundred and fourteen," I told her, twisting the key so she could see for herself.

She gestured grandly around. "Do you see lockers here, flower? No."

She was right. All I could see were heavily laden shelves with barcodes every few inches.

"No lockers at all," she continued, sounding mighty happy about that. "And certainly not one hundred and fourteen of them. Do you have a barcode for me?"

I shook my head, grimacing inwardly.

"No barcode?" She gasped in faux shock. "I can't hand over any property without a barcode." She tapped a notice to the side of me. "Them's the rules, see?"

I did see.

The man waiting directly behind me in the queue cleared his throat.

"Thanks for your help," I told the woman in the booth, determined to be polite in spite of her thinly veiled hostility. After all, I'm British.

"No problem," the woman said, looking over my shoulder. "Can I help you, sir?"

I sidestepped, feeling horribly deflated and a little irritated. I'd had better customer service from goblins! Making my way back to Snitch, who had taken shelter under a winding flight of stairs to my right, I wiggled the key at him. "No joy."

He reached out to take it from me, presumably because he wanted to have another look at it, but our hands collided in mid-air, and I dropped it. It tumbled to the floor and skittered out of our immediate view below the bottom few steps.

"Hell's bells!" Snitch immediately fell to his knees and crawled off after it. I dropped to a crouch and followed him, ready to light my wand if need be to illuminate matters.

"Hello there."

I pulled back in shock. A small man with long,

straggly hair and a pointy beard, already squatting in the darkest part of the space—which wasn't particularly dark—angled his neck to smile at me, green eyes glinting. Older than Snitch by ten or so years, he might have been related in some way. Not that Snitch appeared to know him.

"You're a witch, ain'tcha?" the man asked. He even had the same kind of snuffly laugh as Snitch. "Hehehe. Yeah, I can tell."

"Might be," I said, deciding not to commit until I could figure out what this fellow wanted.

"Yeah you are." He glanced at Snitch. "And you—"

"He's a fine upstanding gentleman." I placed a hand on Snitch's shoulder.

"Huhuhuhuh." Our new friend found that funny. "You looking for this?" He lifted his hand and uncurled filthy fingers. The key rested in the centre of his mucky palm.

"Yes," I said, reaching for it. I half expected him to snatch it away at the last second and make some outrageous demand, a ransom for its return, but he gave it up willingly.

"It's not mine to keep," he said, as though he knew what I was thinking.

"To be honest, it's not exactly ours," I told him.

"It's more yours than theirs."

"Theirs?"

"The people following you."

My back went rigid. I waited a beat before slowly turning my head.

"They're hiding out of sight now," the little man told

me, his tone conversational, as though what we were discussing was of no consequence to either of us. He must have known that was not the case. "They don't want to be seen."

"What do they look like?" I asked.

The little man wobbled his head. "It varies."

"It varies?" I queried, more than a little horrified at the thought.

"The last time I spotted them, they had taken the shape of Metropolitan police officers."

"Shapeshifters?" Snitch whispered, ducking his head.

"That's all we need." I clamped my hand around the key, my heart thumping a little harder in my chest. "Maybe we'd better get out of here."

"It don't matter where you go," the little man told me. "They'll find you."

"But I'll feel a little safer on home territory." I stepped away.

He held up his palm to stop me. "I can take you to the locker if you like."

"The locker that this key will fit?"

He nodded. "Yep."

"I don't want to put you out," I said. What I meant was I didn't want to place him in harm's way.

He tapped his nose, just as Snitch tended to do. "Don't fear. I knows the back ways. The down-and-out ways."

I glanced at Snitch, wondering what he would do in my place. Probably sprint back to the office and heat up his supper.

"What's your name?" I asked the little man.

"Archey."

"Archie? Like Archibald?"

"No, Archey. E and y at the end. Like someone who hides in the railway arches."

Of course.

"I'm Elise," I told him. "This is Snitch."

Snitch sniffed, and the two of them bumped fists. "Pleasure," said Snitch.

Archey nodded over my shoulder. "I see them. They're coming. We should make ourselves scarce."

"We'll follow you," I said, not daring to look behind me.

He ducked through to the other side of the stairs, where there was a slim gap between the glass railing and the wall. The public conveniences were located a little further along, and he aimed straight for them. I imagined we would go inside and make our escape through a window. Instead of that, he darted for a door labelled 'Staff Only'—or what I assumed to be the cleaner's cupboard—and in one small, practised movement, unlocked the door and slipped inside, Snitch at his heels. I didn't think twice. I made a dive for the doorway myself and pulled it closed behind me.

Not a cupboard at all. A dimly lit corridor, the floor and walls tiled in the exact same municipal style, with white squares that reflected what little light there was. The corridor led to a staircase, other doors—storerooms perhaps—opening off this main thoroughfare.

Archey locked the door and beckoned us on. "Hurry," he whispered. Snitch and I quickly fell in behind him. Like Snitch, he strolled rapidly and smoothly, making little noise, without calling any attention to himself. They were silent, while my old Dr Martens squeaked a little every time I took a step.

When we reached the staircase, Archey swung around the newel and began to descend. "Quick!" he urged. We increased our pace. From above and behind me I heard the clatter of a door being thrown open. It might have been our pursuers; it might not have been. I didn't intend to hang around long enough to find out.

We must have climbed down three or four levels—we were moving so fast I lost count—well below ground level. I hadn't realised the station was so deep. "Down here," Archey whispered, and finally we abandoned the stairs and hurried along another corridor, similar to the first one, with more doors off it. But this time, when Archey unlocked the door, we weren't on the concourse but in a lengthy, arched tunnel, slightly reminiscent of the tube tunnels that ran close by.

"It's for access," Archey explained, locking the door behind him.

"Where did you get the keys from?" I asked, gasping slightly from the exertion. Neither Snitch nor Archey were out of breath. Maybe they were used to running away from danger.

"Key." Archey held it up. It was a gold implement, not much like any key I'd ever seen before. It had little wards, clefts and bits running in every direction. "I had a wizard friend run it up for me. Specially designed to open almost any door in the station. Works a treat."

"Why would you—" I started to ask, but Snitch

elbowed me and I zipped my mouth tight. It was like that, was it?

"It comes in useful—" Archey broke off, listening, nose in the air. "Come on."

Without another word, we were off again, but not far. Archey suddenly took a dive to his left into a recessed doorway. With a click, he'd gained access to another stairwell. The door closed behind me and locked automatically, and then we were climbing the stairs—much harder than coming down them—before a swell of noise nearly knocked me backwards. A roar of diesel engines, a scream of metal, a whoosh of warm diesel fumes scented the air.

We'd come out on a platform at the furthest end of the station. A massive Intercity train to our right waited to enter service. Uniformed staff members were on board, getting it ready for passengers.

"We need to be quick." Archey tugged me along the platform, and we ran, fast, as though we were about to miss our train, pushing through people dawdling or loitering around, waiting for the train's doors to open.

Finally, I realised where we were going. Towards the end of the platform was a wall of battered lockers with blue doors. Several dozen of them. Skidding to a halt in front of them, Archey held out his hand for the key. "Number fourteen, wasn't it?" he asked.

"A hundred and—oh!" I realised, like a fool, that the one stood for platform one. I fumbled in the pocket of my jeans, struggling to locate it. It wasn't there! I panicked, fearing for a moment that I'd lost it somewhere between here and the concourse, which bizarrely, wasn't a million miles away from where we were standing. We'd come a long way around to get where we were, but we'd evaded ticket inspectors, security guards and the shapeshifting police officers in the process.

"Jacket pocket." Snitch pointed to my right. I dipped my hand inside and found it there.

Thank the goddesses!

All of them.

Archey took the key and slipped it into the keyhole. It fitted like a glove. One swift twist and he could pull the door of number fourteen open. A pound coin clunked down onto a little cupped shelf in exchange for the return of the key. He reached out and scooped it up, stashing it inside his pocket before anyone—me—could say anything.

"For services rendered," he said.

Snitch nodded his approval.

With a grandiose sweeping gesture, Archey indicated the locker and stepped to his left. I took his place and peered inside. At first I thought it was empty, but then I noticed a small flat object. I reached in to pull it out, and it reacted to my energy by sparkling. I scooped it up. A book.

Like a notebook.

When I flicked through it, the pages were old.

But they were blank.

Snitch leaned closer to me. "What?" he squawked. "Aw! All that for nothing?"

I double-checked the locker, sweeping my free hand around, searching the corners, just to make sure there was nothing else hidden away that I needed to be aware of.

I wasn't as disappointed as Snitch.

I'd seen something similar before.

Archey scuttled sideways. "You've got company," he said.

"What do you mean *you've* got company?" I asked, casting a hasty look behind me, not seeing what he was seeing. "What about you?"

"It's the end of the line for me," Archey said. "Job's a good'n. You got what you was after."

"But how do we get out of here?" I asked. We were trapped on a platform, and the only exit was either along the railway line—which I was certain would cause a huge fuss and lead to the cancellation or at least severe delay of every train in the British Isles—or back along the platform to the concourse, where every person we encountered would be a potential murderer.

"I'm sure you'll come up with something," he said and, waving, took to his heels back the way we had come.

I stuffed the book down the front of my shirt, wedging it between my skin and my bra, then turned to regard the other people on the platform. Overhead a voice boomed out, informing the whole of London that the train currently standing on platform one was ready for boarding. A chorus of beeps sounded as the doors opened.

There was a flurry of movement as travellers began to board the train. I stood where I was, scrutinising the throng. Men. Lots of men. Women. Students. Teenagers.

Kids. Women with pushchairs—not many of them—or carrying babies in arms.

Nobody that looked suspicious.

I looked for pairings.

Two women lugging huge suitcases.

Couples.

A pair of bearded men with walking canes and top hats.

Two student types wearing matching striped bobble hats.

A genuine pair of identical twin girls aged about six, distinguishable only because one clutched a pink rabbit and the other a brown bear.

My gaze returned to the bearded men with the walking canes. Unlike almost everyone else, they were heading down the platform towards us. I flicked a quick look at the train. We were standing beside first class. It was entirely feasible this pair wanted to travel in style. Yet—

Hadn't I seen them before somewhere?

I cast my mind back.

The overhead tannoy announced the imminent departure of the train on platform one.

The bearded men did not alter their pace. They carried on, walking in unison, canes swinging at their side. Their feet, clad in smart boots, click-clacked on the surface of the platform.

Click-clack. Click-clack.

That sound. The sound of two people walking towards me, relentlessly heading my way. Not with any great urgency.

Click-clack. Click-clack.

I reached out slowly, feeling for Snitch's arm.

It came to me in a rush. I'd seen these two men earlier this evening. When I'd come out of the Chinese takeaway.

"Stand clear of the doors on platform one. This train is ready for departure."

The doors began to beep again, the button lights flashing, signifying the imminent locking of the doors. Once the doors had locked, they could not be opened, no matter how much you thumped the buttons to seek access.

"Stand clear of the doors on platform one. This train—"

That was enough for me. There was no going forwards or backwards. We had to go sideways. With one huge effort, I yanked Snitch with me as I rushed for the nearest train door. I thumped the button—fortunately still flashing—as hard as I could. The doors beeped and opened. I jumped up and threw myself into the vestibule; Snitch, not one to be left behind, came in after me. Quick as a flash, I smacked the button again. The doors closed smoothly, and the button's light went out.

They'd locked.

A pair of faces, expressions immovable, appeared at the window, staring in at me. One of the gentlemen smacked his hand against the glass, and both Snitch and I involuntarily jolted backwards. The train shuddered as the brakes were released, almost knocking us off balance, before beginning its effortless glide out of the station. The men with top hats walked alongside us for a few seconds, but, as we picked up speed, they fell away.

I placed my hand on my chest, checking the book was safe.

That had been too close for comfort.

CHAPTER 17

"**W**hoa, DC Liddell, that was close," Snitch said, clutching my arm. "I thought we was goners. Where are we going, anyway?"

"I have no idea." Back in the day, the conductor would have stuck little paper notices on the window of every door so you could check which stations the train would call at. Now you had to read the digital displays. From where we were standing, I couldn't see one. "Wherever we're going, we're going to need to get off again as soon as possible."

I didn't fancy getting on another train and reversing my journey, though. Knowing our luck, our friendly bearded men with the top hats would be waiting for us to arrive back into London.

Snitch wobbled. "Ooh, I ain't got me sea legs yet."

"This is a train, not a boat," I reminded him.

"Well, I ain't never been on neither, so it's all much of a muchness to me."

I felt the hand on my arm tremble. Was Snitch scared? Probably more of the train itself than running away from the shifters.

"We should find a seat somewhere," I said. "At least temporarily."

"Yeah." There was a definite shake to Snitch's voice.

I led him into the nearest carriage, fortunately not too crowded, and we sat opposite each other, with me taking the rearward-facing seat. I didn't want Snitch to completely freak out.

"Tea or coffee, madam? Sir?" A steward dressed in black trousers, maroon waistcoat and a crisp white shirt appeared at my elbow.

"Coffee would be lovely," I said. Something stronger would have been better.

"Tea please, thank you, sir." Snitch sounded quite faint.

The steward deposited our drinks on the table. "Sugar?" he enquired.

"Please," I said.

"Lots," Snitch said. "Really lots. If you don't mind. Please."

The steward smiled, deposited eight straws of sugar on the table and added a couple of mini-packets of biscuits for good measure.

"Cor." Snitch rallied at the sight.

I studied the digital display above the door. We'd managed to board a train to Nottingham. The first stop was Luton, approximately thirty or so miles north of London.

Marvellous.

I stared at my reflection in the window as the lights of the city whizzed past. The brake lights of traffic glowed red as people waited in traffic jams. On the streets I could see ordinary folk attending to their ordinary lives, going about their business, dropping off children at clubs, heading to the pub, shopping and so on. I'd bet that none of them were running away from trouble the way we were.

I tapped the book pressing against my chest for reassurance once more. I had to assume that the men who had chased us through St Pancras were after what we'd found, and if they wanted it, they had to know what it was. If that was the case, they knew far more than I did. I also had to presume they weren't going to stop chasing us just because we'd escaped on a train. It wouldn't take a genius to figure out that we would alight at one of the stops between London and Nottingham.

The question had to be; would they be waiting for us? Would they have sent their cronies to ambush us? Would we recognise the danger when it came?

"It's a bit like being on holiday, isn't it DC Liddell?" Snitch had settled into his seat and was blowing on his drink to cool it down. I noted from the small screwed up wads of paper that he had availed himself of all the sugar. No wonder he didn't have any teeth.

I couldn't think of anything less like being on holiday than having to run for my life, but before I could respond, the door swooshed open behind me.

"Tickets and passes, please!"

Snitch jolted upright, spilling some of his tea down

the front of his robes. "DC Liddell—" he said, eyes wide with fear. "There's a man in a uniform—"

"Calm down. It's fine." I understood where he was coming from, mind. In Tumble Town, people with uniforms were scary beings, often despised and castigated. Scarier for many residents, in fact, than the worst witches and wizards that hid among them. "I'll handle it."

Snitch slumped deeper into his seat and pulled the hood of his robes over his face.

Prising my purse free of a pocket, I turned to face the ticket inspector. "No tickets?" he asked me, giving Snitch the once-over.

"No," I admitted. "Sorry about that."

"How did you get through the barrier?" he asked. "Admittance to the platform is via ticket only. That's not supposed to happen."

"Erm, it was a little unconventional. We only decided to travel at the last second."

The absolute last second.

"Just so you understand, I can only sell you a peak fare?"

I nodded.

"So, where are you headed?"

Decision time. "Luton," I said, pointing at Snitch. "Two please."

"Return?"

"One way."

The ticket inspector tapped his little machine and worked it out. "Sixty-one eighty, please."

"How much?" I exclaimed. "It's only a few miles!"

The ticket inspector pursed his lips. "You're sitting in first class, madam."

Hence the free tea and coffee. *Good goddess!*

I yanked my bank card out of my purse. "I'd like a receipt, please," I growled. At least I could claim the journey back on expenses.

"Of course."

Once we'd exchanged paper and plastic, he moved off down the carriage. "You can come out now," I told Snitch, and he peeped out.

"That was a lot of money," he whispered.

"You're not kidding." I pushed my share of the 'complementary' biscuits his way. "Here, enjoy your holiday."

It took just over forty minutes to arrive into Luton. Snitch and I joined the throng of people—there were loads of them—alighting and hurried after them. Everyone walked comically fast: busy people keen to make it home, to eat, perhaps have a drink, watch a bit of television, sleep and then rise stupidly early the next morning to do it all over again. We climbed the stairs to the bridge and crossed over, trotting down into the foyer, past the ticket machines, and made our way out the front of the neatly kept station.

The taxi rank was just in front of us. A straggly queue stretched ten yards or so.

I glanced around, staring at faces, seeking anyone who might be looking out for us. In the artificial light people appeared tired, focused not on us but only on getting away.

But we wanted to get away too. Back to safety.

We joined the back of the queue. I felt antsy, but I didn't want to alarm Snitch, who was already deep in unchartered waters and had started to twitch if anyone so much as looked at him. "I need a lie-down," he told me.

He wasn't the only one. "Just keep your eyes peeled for anything unusual," I murmured, talking quietly, aware that other travellers were likely to overhear our conversation.

The line of taxis that had been waiting in front of the station began to pull away, availability rapidly exhausted as demand exceeded supply. I turned a complete circle, slowly scanning those around me, then focused on those still exiting the station. Once or twice my heart leapt when I spotted pairs of people who looked alike or who seemed overly couply, but in each case it was a false alarm.

Another half dozen cabs appeared in front of us. We inched slowly forwards and I found myself willing passengers to journey in groups, but, for the most part, everyone in the queue was travelling solo.

Taking a breath, I scrunched up my shoulders and let them drop then wiggled my head, trying to ease out some stress. Across the road from us, looking directly our way, I could see a pair of familiar faces. I froze. The silver-haired women from Bert's market stall. I'd been right. There had been something suspicious about them.

I reached inside my leather jacket and drew out my wand. Snitch noticed the movement straight away.

"Uh-oh," he said.

"Stay sharp, Snitch," I whispered. "They're there. Right in front of us. Do you see?"

"Those old dears?" he queried. "They look quite sweet."

"Yep. But I imagine they could do us some damage. Keep your head down."

We shuffled forwards with the queue as another taxi appeared. We were second in line. As it pulled up beside the portly gentleman in front of us, I clenched my jaw and directed my wand at him. "*Bottomless pockets*," I suggested.

All at once the lining of his pockets unravelled. The change he kept there began to run down the inside of his trouser legs and scatter on the pavement. Pound coins and tuppences, pennies and fifty pences—everything—headed for the gutter and a nearby drain.

Snitch, bless his daft heart, instinctively bent over to help the man pick up his money.

"No time for that," I hissed and yanked the rear door of the taxi open, throwing him inside. Jumping in after him, I reached over to slam the lock down on his side of the car and then my own.

"Drive!" I told the driver.

"Drive where?" he asked, but released the handbrake anyway. We began to move away from the front of the station. I saw the old women take a step off the pavement on their side.

"Towards London," I said, resisting the urge to tell him to step on it. I waited for him to moan about making a journey of that length at this time of night, but he didn't seem to mind. A fare is a fare, and a journey of that length would offer him a decent return, I suppose.

Speaking of which, this was going to cost me an arm and a leg! If I'd imagined the train fare was expensive …

"You do take card, do you?" I asked.

He met my eyes in the rear-view mirror. "Are you kidding, love? We take everything! Card. Bank transfer. PayPal. You name it!"

How very modern. "Great."

I peeked over my shoulder. The station was already fading away in the distance; I could no longer see the old women. Sure, they could follow us, but they couldn't get to us for now. Not right at this second. We'd be safe until we arrived back in Celestial Street.

"It's so fast," Snitch moaned. We were only doing thirty, if that.

I faced the front again and nudged him. "Do your seatbelt up." He was clutching at the door handle as we rounded a corner, completely unnerved by the movement of the car, so different to that of a train.

"What's a seatbelt?" He sounded confused. I showed him mine and he fumbled for his. "Are we going home?"

I hoped he wasn't feeling carsick. This could be an extraordinarily long trip.

To hell with sounding like an extra in a bad movie. "Can you step on it?" I asked the driver.

And he obliged.

We arrived into Celestial Street—via the bookshop in Charing Cross Road—at around quarter past midnight. The clock on the top of the Ministry of Witches was chiming to notify us of the quarter hour. All told, what should have been a relatively short outing had taken us the whole evening. I experienced a wave of relief to be on home territory, but as we wound our way through the overburdened bookshelves in the shop and exited onto the main road, that feeling diminished.

Snitch had a spring in his step and set off towards the entrance to Cross Lane, but I grabbed hold of his robes and pulled him back into the doorway.

"Not so fast, partner."

"What—"

I held up a finger to shush him. "Look around," I said. "You're good at this observing stuff. Tell me what you see."

He pushed back against me, manoeuvring us both into the deepest recess of the doorway. There was a lot of light. The shops were still open, and their gay displays were brilliantly lit. But as with Tumble Town, the streetlights were powered by gas and were given to flickering. They cast long shadows and did little to alleviate the gloomy corners.

There were plenty of beings around. Witches, wizards, goblins, mages, sages, soothsayers—you name it—were out and either doing their weekly shop and picking up essential supplies, or buying treats. The most fantastic smell emanated from a nearby pie shop, and I half expected Snitch to subtly comment on it, but perhaps he was looking forward to finishing his Chinese food because he refrained.

If I'd imagined he would ask me questions about who or what we were searching for, he didn't do that either. He simply ... observed. And he did it in such a subtle way that anybody watching us wouldn't have known he was watching them in return. His eyes were cast down slightly but occasionally flicked right or left or ahead. I would sense him pondering before he turned his attention elsewhere.

A group of seven or eight rabble-rousers tumbled out of The Full Moon Inn, evidently the worse for wear.

"Ten more bottles of beer, please, landlord!" one of them sang, most tunefully.

"Ten more bottles of beer!" The others joined in. "Pop the lid off, we'll swallow them down, then we'll chip in and buy one more round!"

"Over there, DC Liddell," Snitch whispered, pointing at the drunks.

I studied them all, half men, half women, all sizes and shapes, but couldn't immediately see who he meant.

He looped his finger in the air. "Beyond the big group, just coming out of the inn."

I looked beyond the obvious and there, navigating the uneven cobblestones at the front of the building, tagging along with the bigger group and yet somehow not part of it, were a familiar-looking man and woman. A large rotund woman, her peroxide hair curly, her cheeks round, her eyes glassy. Her companion was an equally round man, bald, a little shorter than her. The last time I'd seen them, I'd arrested them for brawling in the street at the site of a murder in Packhorse Close. I hadn't assumed their guilt at that time, just taken their statement at face value that they were attempting to roll a drunk.

But after they'd been released on bail, and their potential involvement in the murders had been discovered, we'd found—or rather DCI Wyld and his team had, because it had been on *their* watch—that they'd given us a false address.

"The Tweedles," I told him. "Do you know them?"

"I know of them," he said. "Martha and Mo. Bad people."

So their reputation preceded them.

"In what way?"

Snitch gave a low whistle. "I've heard you don't want to provoke them. There's stories about a couple of guys who crossed them. One was found hanging from a boat's mast on Dead Man's Wharf, and the other was minced up and fed to pigs at Little Tumble Farm."

Tumble Town had a farm? Who knew?

"Nice," I said.

"Oh, there's plenty of tales I could tell, but I don't know the truth of 'em," Snitch said. "You need to keep out of their way, right enough. That's what I do."

I kept my eyes fixed on them. Any casual observer might have assumed they'd imbibed a little too much goodwill and hospitality, that they were attempting to roll home and that they were simply a pair of harmless old soaks. But to me, and my suspicious nature, their movements were studied; they clutched at each other, giggled and linked arms. Their attention was elsewhere, seemingly on each other, but inch by inch they were moving directly towards us.

Then they disappeared.

I caught my breath. "What? Where did they go?"

"Over there, DC Liddell."

Reluctantly, I shifted my gaze and followed Snitch's nod. Over by the entrance to Cross Lane, too far away to make out any specific characteristics, if that wasn't my pair of silver-haired old ladies, I'd eat Ezra's trilby.

I tutted in annoyance. On the one hand, it paid to be vigilant; on the other, it now seemed that any potential exit was blocked. "Is there an army of people following us?"

I'd assumed that I wouldn't be able to make it into Tumble Town and that trying to make my way to Wonderland, which was where I wanted to end up, would be too risky, but the alternative route—visiting my ex-colleagues at the MOWPD—was also potentially cut off if our foes could move that quickly.

These people—whoever they were—were smart. They knew exactly what I'd try to do. And they had the capability to outmanoeuvre me.

But in that case, perhaps it was time to do something unexpected.

I gripped Snitch's elbow. "We can't stay here," I told him. "We'll make a move in the opposite direction."

"But that's towards the hospital and the park. We'll be out in the open—"

He wouldn't be able to hide. He would hate that. "And there won't be so many witnesses around, I know that."

"They'll easily track us if we go that way—"

"We won't be going too far. Follow me and stay close, okay?"

"Okay."

"Walk fast, but don't run." I stepped out of the doorway. The old ladies had gone, but the Tweedles had reappeared, closer now. The woman met my eye, her guard falling for just a second, her lip curling with a malevolence I found unnerving. She leaned over to Mr Tweedle and mouthed something. They dropped all pretence of drunkenness and started towards us.

"Let's go," I said, swivelling in the opposite direction. Snitch didn't need telling twice. He slipped alongside me, keeping to the shadows wherever he could. We kept up a brisk pace without looking back, listening out for encroaching footsteps that would alert us to the fact that the Tweedles were right on our tail.

At the point where Celestial Street ended, I reached out and hoiked Snitch to our right. There were several rows of terraces here, early twentieth-century houses constructed with yellow brick, neat and built to last. Each was the same as its neighbour. A bay window and a front door behind a low wall with iron railings. A tiny front garden, only big enough for a few container plants and a black bin, a step up and you were inside. Unlike the terraces in Tumble Town, these were roomy. A good-sized front room, kitchen and dining room to the rear. A hallway leading up to three bedrooms and a bathroom.

We clattered along at a decent pace. There were no cobbles here, only tarmac, although the pavement had seen better days and needed resurfacing. The street was quiet. The residents here tended to work at the Ministry of Witches, for the witches' civil service, at the hospital or university and academies. Professionals.

"Where are we going?" Snitch asked.

"Save your breath," I told him, although once again, it was me who was feeling it, not him.

Something clanked behind us, and I twisted my head to steal a peek. The Tweedles, advancing on us, moving at a fair lick.

"Come on!" I broke into a jog. Ahead of us, a hundred yards or so, was a pub. We needed to get just beyond that.

"Ohhhh," Snitch complained. It seemed he objected to having to run. "We're going the wrong way!"

For Tumble Town, yes, but that wasn't our destination.

"Not far," I panted.

Fifty yards to go.

Forty.

Thirty.

I could read the sign outside the pub now. *'England game here on the big screen on the eleventh!'* it announced.

Twenty yards.

Snitch made the mistake of glancing behind him. We were moving too fast, and the pavement was uneven. He caught his toe on the edge of the pothole and fell forwards.

I reached out to try and grab him, but it all happened too quickly. He went sprawling, putting his hands out to save himself, sliding painfully along the ground.

I had to stop to help him up. I could hear the approaching footsteps echoing around the empty street. I reached for Snitch and hauled him to his feet. Thank goodness there was so little of him. He limped a few steps. "Ow!"

"Come on!" I urged him.

"Go on without me," he cried. Truly pitiful, in fact.

"This isn't a blooming democracy, Snitch. Move it!"

Tugging him forwards, practically dragging him, we made it to the pub. I could see the house I was looking for, but Snitch was labouring. He genuinely had hurt himself.

"Can't we hire a donkey?" he asked.

"We're here!" I told him. "You can do it! Lean on me!"

He did so, to the extent that I practically carried him the last few yards before I could deposit him on the step. Behind us, the Tweedles had reached the pub.

I smacked my hand against the door. Hard. I could see a light on inside, I just had to pray that the occupant was home and hadn't simply left it on as a security measure. There was no guarantee.

All was quiet. The Tweedles ambled towards us. The woman's eyes glowed with an eerie light; the man's neck stretched to see what would happen.

I smacked the door harder. It vibrated beneath my stinging hand. "Open up!" I shouted.

Bang. Bang. Bang!

"Come on!"

The Tweedles were fifteen yards from us.

"Hurry, DC Liddell!" Snitch cried.

"Let me in!" I thumped the door again.

Finally, I heard noise from beyond the door. The outside light came on above my head and I heard the safety chain pulled clear.

"Liddell?"

"Yes!"

The door opened a crack, and Monkton's bleary eye blinked out at me. "Do you have any idea what time it is?"

"Let us in!" I pushed at the door.

"Us?" He opened the door a little wider so he could look out. "Who's us?"

"Me and Snitch!" I helped Snitch to his feet.

"You can't bring a convict in here," Monkton hissed. "What will my superiors think?"

"I'm not a convict!" Snitch protested. "I was found innocent of all wrongdoing."

"You never went to court; therefore you were never acquitted of any charges." Monkton stood his ground. "You confessed!"

"Shut up and let us in!" I roared.

"Sssh! You're going to wake my neighbours, Liddell!" Monkton grumbled.

"There are people after us! Let. Us. IN!" I pushed against the door once more.

Monkton opened it but stepped out rather than let us in. He was wearing a pair of blue cotton shorts and a black t-shirt with an image of Duke Ellington embla-zoned across the chest.

He frowned. "What people?"

I turned to jab my finger at the Tweedles. But the street was empty.

They'd evaporated into the night.

CHAPTER 18

"This had better be good, Liddell." Monkton led us into his front room, dominated by an old piano. He had an old-fashioned stacking hi-fi, and soft jazz floated out of enormous floor speakers. Little lights shone across the room, reflected from the record player, where a vinyl record spun endlessly, a laser picking out the mirrors on the spinning turntable.

You could tell Monkton was a bachelor. The room was clean but untidy; one whole wall had been given over to shelves that housed his vinyl collection. A gigantic television had been mounted on the wall above the fireplace. A few bedraggled ferns in pots—badly in need of watering—were littered around for decoration. He had a worn but comfortable three-piece suite grouped around a scarred coffee table laden with his work files and a couple of thick biographies that he may or may not have been reading. The overall effect was cosy and lived-in.

It looked as though he'd fallen asleep listening to

music. A couple of cushions lay on the floor next to the sofa, and the multicoloured crocheted throw was ruffled. A bottle of beer—almost full—was placed close by on the floor.

Monkton moved to pick that up, and chucked the cushions back on the sofa while he was at it.

"You may as well make yourself at home." He took a swallow of his beer and grimaced. "Temporarily. I'd offer you one of these, but I'm going to assume you'll make this snappy and get out of my hair."

"I hate to disappoint you," I told him, "but I don't think we'll be going anywhere tonight."

"And I hate to disillusion you, but I've only been home an hour and I have to get back to the office by seven. I need my beauty sleep."

Snitch hovered by the door, his face pale. I took his arm and helped him to one of the armchairs. "Take your boot off," I told him. "I want to see."

"Owww, I'll be alright, DC Liddell. Don't you worry—"

"You know what would be nice?" I put my hands on my hips and glared first at Snitch and then at Monkton. "If everyone would stop arguing with me when I know better! You!" I jabbed my finger at Snitch. "Take the boot off! And *you*"—I glowered at Monkton—"need to understand that we're not going anywhere until daylight."

"But—" They both began to argue at once.

"End of." I stormed towards Monkton, snatched the bottle from his hand and necked it myself—down in one—before handing the empty back to my old boss.

"Right." Monkton ruffled his hair with his free hand. "I thought you were on the wagon. Do you want another one?"

"Please."

"What about—" He gestured with the bottle in Snitch's direction.

"Yes, he will," I answered for him, staring down at Snitch's foot, the skin yellow, the nails on his toes like talons. Even from this distance I could see the swelling of his ankle. "And bring some ice if you've got any."

A couple of minutes later, Snitch had a cold compress—ice wrapped in a tea towel—to apply to his foot, and a cold beer to help ease the discomfort. He sat, shyly hunched, in Monkton's armchair, avoiding the DCI's gaze.

"Well?" Monkton asked. He looked a little more awake now. Long nights on duty, or sudden awakenings at home, were a big part of his job. Something I was glad I didn't have to deal with anymore.

I unzipped my leather jacket and carefully eased the notebook out from beneath my t-shirt. I lay it gently on the table. It sparkled at every point my fingers touched it, something that appeared to be lost on Monkton.

"It's a notebook, Liddell." Monkton shrugged. He reached out and flipped the cover. The title page was blank. He riffled through the pages. All blank. "There's nothing in it."

"It belonged to Annie Mendoza. Or Lily Rose Budd," I told him.

It was his turn to look annoyed. "You found this at

her flat? I've had a team in there tearing the place apart this evening."

"Not in the flat." I did my best to appear apologetic. "I trust Wootton sent through copies of the documents I found?"

"The passport and photos? Yes. I received the copies. I want the originals."

"Of course, you can have them." I tried to smooth things over. "So, you'll know she was Special Branch?"

Monkton huffed a sigh. "We got that far, yes. But so far I've drawn a blank on what she was investigating."

"Us too."

"It's not your case, Liddell!"

I waved his concerns away. "Besides the passport and the photos, there was a bundle of notes—"

"Your assistant sent through details of those, too." Good old Wootton, covering my back. "I've traced the serial numbers; they're legit. Notes that were already in circulation. Nothing dodgy about them."

"Just getaway cash," I agreed. "In case of emergencies."

"Why would she need to make an emergency getaway?" Monkton asked.

"She was working undercover," I told him. "I've been doing a bit of background research, and it seems she was watching a business on Tetris Alley. Wasted Youth Tattoos?"

I waited for him to put two and two together. It took him a while. I could see the cogs turning, too slowly for my liking. But I suppose it was late in the evening. Or early in the morning, depending on your take.

"The place where you ran into a spot of bother before?"

Nothing like underselling the trouble I'd been in. Wootton and I had come close to being barbequed.

"That's the place." I took a swig of my beer and wiped my mouth. "Did Wootton send you an image of the key we found?"

"No-oooo." Monkton shook his head. "What key?"

"To a left luggage locker. We tracked it down to St Pancras." I waved away his questions. "This was what we found. It was the *only* thing in the locker."

"A blank notebook? I don't get it."

He could be frustratingly slow on the uptake sometimes.

"I'm hazarding a guess that there's material in this notebook that would be extremely damaging to the Labyrinthians."

"Oh, not this again, Liddell." Monkton sat back and rolled his eyes. "You're obsessed. You know I try to fight your corner with my superiors, but they're getting a bit tired of your insinuations that we don't know what we're doing. They're losing patience and taking it out on me."

"Is that what *you* think I think? That *you* don't know what *you're* doing?"

"It comes across that way, sometimes." Monkton shifted uncomfortably. "Ibeus—"

"Never mind Ibeus! She doesn't have her ear to the ground. She has no idea what's going on. She's too hands-off. She's—"

"My incredibly irate boss!"

"It's not that I don't think you can do the job." *Albeit slowly.* "I know you can! It's more that you don't seem to hear me when I talk about this organised crime group."

"There are those who claim you've made the whole thing up." Monkton pulled a face. "I try to defend you—"

"Who says that? Ibeus?" I burned with indignation.

"It's just tittle-tattle at the MOW." Monkton shook his head as though he gave such gossip little credence.

I put the beer he'd given me on the coffee table. I shouldn't be drinking. I needed all my faculties.

"Elise." Monkton sat forward again and patted my hand. "We've been friends and colleagues for many years. In all that time, I never once distrusted your judgement. You're a great detective. Straight. Focused. Intelligent. Fearless. I couldn't ask for more from one of my officers."

I could hear the 'but' coming.

"After we lost Ezra, you went to pieces. Your mental health suffered. I understood. That's why I supported you all the way. I wanted you to take a leave of absence and then, when you were ready, come back to my team. Remember?"

I did.

"You could have availed yourself of any of our counsellors and therapists, had you wanted." He perked up. "Maybe you still could. They offer their services to retired officers too, if I recall correctly."

I gently removed his hand and squeezed it. He meant well. "There's nothing wrong with my mental health now," I told him. "And as for the Labyrinthians—"

He groaned.

"I've told you over and over. The Labyrinthians are real. Cerys Pritchard killed Dodo at someone else's instigation. Dodo is *my* case. This makes this"—I tapped the notebook, watching it shimmer—"*my* business."

"You have to hand it over to me," Monkton said.

I pretended not to hear that. "I'm going to have Wizard Dodo take a look at it."

"You can't," Monkton told me, frowning. "It's evidence in a murder case. We have a forensic team who can run tests."

"We don't need tests," I replied, carrying on doggedly. Would I *ever* make this man understand? "Wizard Dodo can unlock it. Forensics will never be able to do that."

"He's a ghost, Elise."

I laughed. "What difference does that make?"

"He's dead."

"He's still a sentient being!"

"I doubt his evidence will hold up in court. It would be his word against the prosecution, assuming you were ever able to prosecute these Labyrinthians."

"It won't be just *his* word," I said, "because you'll be coming with me to witness him unlocking the book. In fact, bring a friend. Bring a camera. This will all be above board, I promise."

Monkton grunted. "Have you any idea how busy I am? I have five ongoing murder investigations—"

"This is the best lead you have in Annie Mendoza's murder. I'm handing it to you on a plate!"

"It'll be a wild goose chase."

"Argh!" The man was impossible. Did he argue for the sake of it? "It may be something and nothing, but Annie Mendoza was onto something. That's why she was on the marketplace. She was watching people. She was making notes. She knew stuff."

A loud snore interrupted our discussion. I darted a startled look at Snitch. He had fallen asleep in the armchair, slumped over to one side, his head thrown back, his mouth wide open. He snored again, so loudly the windows vibrated.

I lowered my voice, not wanting to wake him. "She knew stuff," I repeated.

Monkton sighed. "It's late. We should get some shut-eye. You can take the spare bed if you like. I'll help your friend to the sofa."

"Don't disturb him," I whispered. "He's probably slept in much worse places than your scruffy old armchair."

"Hey! Don't cast aspersions on my good furniture." He smiled, his good nature restored.

"So will you?" I asked, getting to my feet and grabbing the notebook. I intended to sleep with it under my pillow.

"Will I what?"

"Come to Wonderland tomorrow and watch Dodo unlock this?" I waved the book at him. Sparkles of light flew around us.

"If you think it's worth it." He sighed.

"Annie thought it was."

"And look where that got her."

I rolled my eyes. That was *exactly* the point!

CHAPTER 19

By six thirty the following morning, Monkton was up and freshly dressed in a suit, crisp shirt and tie, and was making tea and toast for everyone. He looked immaculate and smelt gorgeous and didn't seem at all affected by a lack of sleep, while Snitch and I definitely looked the worse for wear.

Overnight, Snitch's ankle had ballooned and taken on a garish rainbow of mustard, purple and blue. I stared aghast, wondering how we would manage to get him back to Wonderland. I considered asking Monkton whether he'd allow Snitch to remain here, but on second thoughts, realised neither he nor Snitch would appreciate that.

Monkton bit into a slice of brown toast and examined the ankle from afar. "You'll live," he said.

"He can't walk on that," I argued.

"I'll be fine, DC Liddell, don't you worry." Snitch pushed himself out of the armchair.

"See!" Monkton said. "If he can stand, he's halfway there."

Halfway where? I wondered. We were nowhere near halfway home! "There's a difference between standing and walking. We might have to move fast, that's my thinking," I explained.

Monkton offered me some toast. "You worry too much. I've asked DC Larch to meet us here."

"Larch?"

"New to my team. A good egg. You said I could bring a witness, after all."

"Yes, but—" I hadn't for a moment imagined he'd take me up on the offer.

"As a bonus, he's built like a tank." He handed the plate of remaining toast to Snitch, who stared down at it as if all his Samhains had come at once. "Think of him as added security. Nothing is going to happen that we can't handle."

Such confidence.

I studied Snitch's foot doubtfully. "Do you at least have something I can bind this up with?" Getting Snitch's boot back on would be a nightmare.

"I've got a first aid kit under the sink in the kitchen. One sec." He darted away, seemingly without a care in the world.

For his part, Snitch was leaving all the worry to me, too. He nibbled delicately on a piece of toast. He had a funny way of eating. That's what came of missing his top front teeth.

Monkton rejoined us and offered me a pile of bandages and tape. "I've twisted ankles and knees numerous times over the years playing five-a-side footy," he said by way of explanation. He nodded at Snitch. "It needs to be tight but not so tight you cut off his circulation."

I knelt down in front of Snitch, wondering how I'd ended up with this particular job. Surely, with all his experience, Monkton would have been the better choice to play nurse. I couldn't be sure of the last time Snitch's feet had seen soap and water—and I wasn't about to ask—and just the sight of his nails made my stomach heave.

"Ow," Snitch grumbled quietly, hanging on to his plate of toast for dear life as I straightened his foot.

"Oh, sorry, Mr Rich! Am I hurting you?" I asked, not even bothering to hide my sarcasm.

Monkton peered over my shoulder as I unravelled a bandage. "I'd leave it rolled up if I were you. It makes it easier to wrap around the joint—"

I glared up at him. "Do you want to do it?"

There was a knock on the front door. Both Snitch and I froze.

"So jumpy," Monkton said. "That'll be Larch."

"Make sure you check before you open the door," I called after him as he disappeared into the hall.

Once he was out of the way, and quick as a flash, I grabbed the notebook from where I'd left it while I'd been having a cup of tea. I nudged Snitch, whose attention remained solely focused on the two halves of toast left on his plate. "I need you to look after this," I told him, my voice hardly audible.

"Me?" he whispered, eyes wide.

"I trust you," I told him, kneeling beside him once more. "Put it somewhere safe."

He stuffed the notebook inside his robes, fiddling for a few moments to secure it inside a pocket within a pocket.

"Listen," I continued, flicking my gaze nervously towards the hallway. Monkton and, presumably, Larch were engaged in a conversation about the upcoming England football match. "If something happens to me—"

"What do you mean?" Snitch asked in alarm.

"Shhh!" I urged him. "Keep your voice down!"

He nodded, his eyes like saucers now.

"Whatever happens, I need this book to get back to Wonderland. You hand it over to Ezra and no-one else. Do you understand?"

Snitch nodded again; his face crumpled as though he were about to burst into tears.

"Ezra needs to talk to Minsk, and they should ask Dodo to read the book. Okay?"

Snitch nodded one final time. "Ezra. Minsk. Dodo. Got it."

"Liddell?" Monkton walked back into the room. "This is DC Larch. DS Izax's replacement."

As if anybody could replace Ezra!

Larch was, as Monkton had insinuated, a tall, broad man. I'd seen him accompany Monkton to several jobs recently. He was recognisable by his shock of red curly hair and pale complexion. In his mid-twenties, he had pale blue eyes and a friendly smile.

Monkton continued his introductions. "This is ex-detective Liddell—no doubt you've heard of her—and her friend, erm, Bartholomew Rich."

"Call him Snitch. Nice to meet you. I would shake hands but, er … I don't know where these've been," I said, gesturing at Snitch's foot.

Snitch blinked. "Oh."

"No offence," I told him.

"Had a bit of an accident, have you?" Larch asked, crouching next to me. "May I?" He reached for the bandage in my hand.

"Be my guest." I shuffled backwards. In no time at all, DC Larch had Snitch's ankle securely bound up, his sock on and his boot laced up. It must have hurt because Snitch lay the toast aside and didn't pick it up again, even when Larch had finished. He simply flopped back in the armchair, looking utterly miserable.

"Good job," I said, pulling on my jacket and zipping it up.

"I did a first aid course at the police academy," he told me. "I had thought about becoming a paramedic."

"I hate to interrupt this little icebreaking session," Monkton complained, "but it's ten past seven and we need to get going. The sooner Liddell gets what she wants, the sooner I can get back to my caseload."

I helped Snitch to his feet. He stepped tentatively forward and winced. "You can do this, Snitch," I told him. "We'll soon be home."

"Allow me." Larch moved to the other side of Snitch. "Place your arm around my middle and use me as a support when you need to step on the ankle." They tried it out. "That's it."

"Splendid," Monkton said. "Let's get going." He pocketed his phone and wallet and grabbed his keys. "Have you got the book, Elise?"

I patted the front of my leather jacket.

We made slow progress along Monkton's road, heading back towards the turning into Celestial Street. His neighbours were up and about, leaving for work. Kids in neat red robes, the uniform of the closest primary school—with freshly combed hair, backpacks and lunchboxes—bounced boisterously around in the company of a relative or guardian, while the road's familiars—cats, dogs, foxes and even a leopard—stretched and ambled around, sniffing out fresh smells. One or two older women swept outside the front of their houses with their broomsticks, eyes hooded, but watching as everyone came and went.

In contrast, Wyld, Larch, Snitch and I made for quite a shambolic grouping. At least Larch and Wyld looked smart, but I hadn't seen a hairbrush for over twenty-four hours, and Snitch? Well, there was no hope. He and Larch stumbled along like the last-placed couple in a three-legged race. Monkton strode ahead, nodding at his neighbours, while I brought up the rear, my wand clenched tightly in one hand, my mobile in the other.

I'd already tried to reach Minsk a few times but had drawn a blank. Wootton wasn't at his desk yet, but Ezra was there, and he took my call. "Where are you?" he asked. "I've been worried sick. I even went over to St

Pancras myself at two this morning to see if I could find you."

"Sorry, I should have let you know I was at Wyld's."

"Oh aye?" I could hear Ezra's imagination working overtime. "I thought you and he—"

"No!" I shut him up before he could go on. "Look. Snitch and I are on our way back, and we may have a bit of trouble."

"Do you want me to come out? Meet you somewhere?"

"Wyld is with me."

I watched my old boss smile cheerfully at a woman with three kids. "Lovely day, isn't it?" he was saying.

"That's good." Ezra didn't seem convinced.

"I'm not sure he truly appreciates the gravity of the situation, but he is with me. He's brought someone else along too, so hopefully we'll be alright. I just wanted to let you know we're on our way."

"Alright." He still didn't sound too sure. "I'll put the kettle on."

"If you can get hold of Minsk, that would be good."

"I'll do my best."

"Cheers."

I broke the connection and stuffed the phone back into my pocket, then hastened forward to catch hold of Snitch's other arm. We were almost on Celestial Street and, while there were people around—mostly those on their way to work—few shops were open yet, and there was none of the bustle you would expect to find in the afternoon and evening.

I was in two minds about that. On the one hand, it

was easier to observe anyone standing around or heading towards us, but on the other, fewer bystanders possibly meant more trouble.

I soon realised how much.

I spotted the silver-haired ladies first, each wearing long black woollen coats over ankle-length skirts. They stepped out of the doorway of a shoe shop to our right. One tracked our every move, her eyes shining with petty spite, the other had her head turned away, slightly cocked as though she were listening out for something.

"Ow!" Snitch jerked in my grasp. I'd squeezed his arm a little too hard.

"Sorry." I loosened my grip and tried to catch Monkton's attention. "Monkton?" I called softly, trying not to alarm anyone else.

He was oblivious. Strolling along without looking back. "Yo, Wyld!"

He stopped and waited for us to catch up. "Over there," I told him, pointing at the women.

Standing alongside me, he followed the direction of my finger. "What am I looking at, Liddell? Those two old dears?" I could tell by the chuckle in his voice he didn't believe they were a threat.

And maybe they weren't. Maybe this was all in my head. But just the way they were looking at us was enough to make my blood run cold. They'd been at Luton station last night. That hadn't been a coincidence.

I turned away from them, peering in the direction of the entrance to Cross Lane. At least that seemed clear. Pushing at Monkton's arm, I said, "Yeah, alright. Whatever. Let's carry on."

But he didn't move, only frowned and took a few steps closer to the shoe shop. "Wait."

I glanced back at the doorway. The women were gone.

"Did you see that?" Monkton asked.

"See what?" I hadn't seen anything. One second they'd been there, the next they'd vanished.

"They faded away." Monkton grimaced. "Did you see that, Larch?"

"I did, sir! Very odd!"

"Dark magick," Snitch muttered. "We should go."

At least that was something we all agreed upon. With Snitch between us, Larch and I practically carried him towards the Cross Lane entrance, but once we were through, the lane immediately became too narrow for us both to walk alongside him. In fact, in places it was virtually impossible to walk two abreast. We carried on the best we could, but eventually I had to fall back and allow Larch to bear Snitch's not particularly significant weight by himself. He could have given him a piggyback and we'd have made better progress, but I doubt Snitch would have enjoyed that.

Up ahead of us, a window opened on the first floor of a squat, narrow house. A second later, the resident emptied out a bucket onto the lane. The contents spattered on the cobbles, narrowly missing Monkton. He jumped back with a shriek of disgust.

As I stared upwards, I observed a large bird alighting on an iron bracket. It cocked its head to stare at me with ill-concealed loathing. Peering up, I could see the sleek black of its feathers. It might have been a crow, apart from the silver sheen on its head.

"Guys—" I started to say, as another one joined it. Identical to the first, this one didn't look at us, but it lifted its beak and cawed loudly. The call echoed from rooftops all around us. Dumbstruck, I observed as dozens of birds swooped into view, darkening the sky above. They fluttered and squawked and fought among each other as they sought a place to perch on the guttering of the old houses. Their heads twisted this way and that to watch us as we shuffled along below them.

People have often described me as fearless, but I have to admit at that moment, my insides turned to liquid. I don't have a problem with birds on the whole. But the sounds above my head, the raucous call and response, the chorus of guttural croaks all caused my spine to turn to jelly. I'd never heard anything like it.

"Ugh!" Larch used his free hand to bat away invisible things from around his head. "I can't bear birds!"

"Keep going," Monkton urged us from up ahead. From the less than confident look on his face, I could see he was feeling the same way. This was not how we expected birds to behave.

Alone at the rear, I ducked under the bracket, keeping a careful eye on the silver-headed twin crows. Wonderland seemed like a long way away. In turn, they eyed me spitefully.

"I don't like this," I murmured.

"Perhaps it would be better to take Paternoster Row," Larch suggested.

"Is that a quicker route?" Monkton wanted to know.

"Not particularly," Larch answered, "but it's covered over. We'll be out of the birds' sight for about eighty yards or so."

"But it will take us out of our way," I argued. "It's the wrong direction."

"It comes out at Silversmith Street. I know a short cut from there," Larch argued. "I just can't stand birds! We can make up time—"

Monkton glanced up just as one of the birds dropped like a stone, heading straight for him. "Eek!" He ducked away, but in the narrow confines of Cross Lane, there was nowhere to go. I levelled my wand at it as, claws extended, it reached for his scalp. *"Mora!"*

The bird exploded in a cloud of feathers.

"Oops." A little too much intent, perhaps. I needed to calm myself.

That made Monkton's mind up. "Lead on," he told Larch, brushing feathers from his lapel and the sleeves of his jacket.

"I honestly don't think—" I tried to intervene.

"Nor me." Even Snitch sounded alarmed, and he knew Tumble Town like the back of his hand, but Larch was already manhandling Snitch into the covered alley, actually more like a long thin tunnel. Paternoster Row had been cleverly constructed, many centuries ago, into an oval-shaped passageway that led from the old monastery. Monkton went after them. Reluctantly, I brought up the rear, still protesting.

"Monkton?" I said, my voice echoing around the

space. "I really think we should go direct to Tudor Lane."

"We're safe in here," Monkton called back. "The birds won't follow us in, and if anyone else comes after us, we'll see them from a long way off." He pointed up ahead. "Look! There's light at the end of the tunnel already."

I'd never travelled along Paternoster Row before, so I had no idea what to expect. It opened out into a court-yard, the sort of cobbled area, complete with fountain, that you might have found in Italy. Ahead of us the imposing exterior of the monastery towered above us, its cold grey stone reminiscent of a French castle, the outer wall topped by the grim or gurning visages of gargoyles. To the left, under an arch, a slightly wider path led out to Silversmith Street—according to the black and white street sign nailed to the wall anyhow. To the right was another small tunnel, rather like Pater-noster Row. This one was not signposted, and I had no idea where it led.

Larch had been right on one score at least: there were no birds here. We'd outfoxed them. But I still couldn't comprehend how heading in the opposite direction to Tudor Lane would help us make up time.

Snitch wriggled away from Larch. "I think I can manage now," he said. "I'll hold onto the wall for a little support." As if to prove his point, he hobbled away from us and rested against the arch, his face twisting in pain.

"Snitch. I don't think—" I started to say, but suddenly things were happening at lightning speed.

Movement in my peripheral vision. I spun on one

foot. A pair of figures emerged from behind the fountain. A large woman. An equally round man.

Martha and Mo Tweedle.

"There!" I alerted Larch and Wyld to their sudden appearance and levelled my wand. Before I could use it, however, Larch had turned his own wand on me.

"*Exarmaueris!*"

A short, sharp beam of energy shot towards me, dislodging the wand from my hand and sending it flying.

"Yow!" I shrieked, clasping my burning hand to my chest, certain my fingers had been dislocated.

Monkton spun on his heel. "DC Larch! What are you—"

Larch didn't give him time to finish. "*Praeligo.*" The binding spell felled Monkton. He dropped to his knees, his mouth twisting in anguish.

"Larch?" Monkton repeated, his voice ragged, before falling forwards and writhing in agony.

I rushed to him, easing him onto his side. "Stay with me," I told him.

"Call for backup," he croaked.

I reached for my phone, but before I could find it, Larch was by my side, his wand pressed against the side of my head. "Make another move and I'll kill you," he said, his voice dripping with acid.

I raised my hands, the right one throbbing in time to my elevated heart rate. "Alright," I said. "Don't do anything foolish."

"Foolish was you imagining you could come after us," Larch sniped.

"Shut it!" Martha Tweedle snapped. "Take her phone then get the notebook."

Larch poked his wand painfully against my temple. I handed my phone over. "Now give me the notebook."

I leaned away from him. If I managed to grab his wand off him, I was going to thrust it, wide end first, up his left nostril and embed it in whatever brain he had. "What notebook?"

He jabbed me again.

"Don't play games," Martha said. "We were there when you found it in the locker last night."

Mo Tweedle grinned. "Thanks for locating it for us."

"I don't know what you mean." I shrugged.

Martha curled her lip. "I don't have time for this. Have it your way." She nodded at Larch. "Kill her little friend."

Larch aimed his wand in the direction of the arch where, only moments before, Snitch had been leaning with one hand against the uneven surface, propping himself up.

"No!" I leapt to my feet, grabbing for Larch's wand. Too late.

A dull whoompf sound. Larch had fired. I closed my eyes as the arch exploded. Smashed to smithereens, detritus from the structure flew in all directions, bigger chunks smacking the ground and slamming into the other walls around us, smaller chips flying everywhere, raining down indiscriminately, stinging my face and hands.

"You fool!" Martha Tweedle was screaming.

I hardly dared to look, but how could I not?

Where Snitch had been standing, there was nothing. No sign of him. Not his robes, not his boots, no body, no body parts.

My head vibrated from the power of the magickal wave, and my mind reeled in shock. They'd killed Snitch! I clutched my stomach, knowing I would retch. It was like losing Ezra all over again. All my fears had come to pass—

Martha Tweedle was beside herself. "He'd already gone, you knucklehead!"

"Gone?" Larch repeated.

"Gone?" I whispered.

"Down Silversmith Street!"

Had Snitch managed to get away? Hope lit up my soul. I sent a million pleases and thank yous to all the goddesses at once. *Run, Snitch, run!*

Or hop, as the case might be.

"Go after him you … you blithering idiot!" Martha raged.

"No." Mo Tweedle found his voice. His gaze shifted to me. I didn't like what I saw there. Something dark and pitiless. "The weasely one is of no consequence to us. Just get the book."

Larch glanced uncertainly between the Tweedles, unsure which of them to obey. I considered making a run for it myself, but that would mean leaving Monkton on his own and in any case, I wasn't sure I would get very far.

"You heard the boss," Larch said. "Hand the book over."

I shook my head. "Good work on coming across as

an amiable colleague. Someone DCI Wyld could trust. Affable and genial. Someone even I would have liked to have worked with once upon a time." And to think he was Ezra's replacement? No chance.

"Cut the crap and give me the book." He shifted the direction of his wand from me to Wyld. "You know what I'm capable of, so let's have no more nonsense."

I slowly raised my hands, palms up, considering my options. I needed to stall them. If Snitch had managed to get away—may it please all the goddesses—then I needed to allow him time. Plenty of time, given the state of his ankle.

The problem was, the Tweedles weren't messing around.

"You get one more chance," Mo Tweedle was saying, regarding me cannily as though he could read my mind. If I'd thought him the more stupid of the two, I couldn't have been more wrong. "If you mess us around any longer, we'll slice chunks off the police officer while you watch. Then when we're done with him, we'll start on you."

Martha chortled and clapped her hands. "Oh, how delightful!"

The male Tweedle nodded curtly but didn't take his eyes from me. "Glad you approve."

Needless to say, I didn't.

I regarded Monkton, still prone on the floor. How could I help him and help myself?

"Time's up!" Mo Tweedle had finally had his fill of my procrastination.

I reached down and began to unzip my jacket.

Slowly, slowly, inch by inch, taking my time as though I didn't want to alarm them, I pulled it wide so they could see I wasn't hiding anything.

Time to break the bad news.

"You're out of luck," I told them. "I don't have it anymore."

Mo rounded on Martha. "We saw it with our own eyes."

She nodded. "She had it!" She pointed at Larch. "Search her."

He did so, in the time-honoured tradition of the trained police officer. "Why are you working for those people?" I asked him. "What did they offer you?"

"They're not 'those' people, they're *my* people."

"They're responsible for the death of police officers," I reminded him. "You can't honestly live with that?"

He refused to answer. When he'd finished checking me over—even down to the inside of my boots—he shook his head at the Tweedles. "She must have left it in Wyld's house. I can go back—"

He got no further. Mo Tweedle lifted his hand and threw a finger out in a sharp gesture. Larch caught his breath and dropped like a stone to the ground beside Monkton. He lay there, face down, not moving at all.

I gasped.

They'd killed him. Just like that.

They're *my* people, he'd said.

I could only thank my lucky stars they weren't mine.

Shaken, I nevertheless focused on maintaining my composure. I couldn't let the Tweedles sense any fear on my part. "That's better," I said. "It's two against two now."

Martha Tweedle snorted, pointing at Monkton. "He's hardly in a position to help you out."

"No. But I am."

The male voice came from behind them. Above our heads.

I squinted upwards at a shape atop the monastery's outer wall. It was pushing against one of the heavier gargoyles. The resulting grinding noise set my teeth on edge. The shadow darted from view, and the gargoyle began to inch forward, seemingly of its own volition. It teetered on the edge for what felt like an eternity, but in reality was a fraction of a second.

"Run, Elise!" the anonymous voice from above ordered. The gargoyle had reached the point of no return.

I could run. Sure.

But I wouldn't leave Monkton to die here alone.

CHAPTER 20

I threw myself forward to cover Monkton as the gargoyle crashed to earth in the centre of the courtyard, splintering into a thousand pieces. In doing so, I temporarily lost sight of the Tweedles, but that was the last thing I was worried about. Once again I was showered in fragments of carved stone and dust. It stung, but fortunately we were far enough away from the impact that there was nothing substantial enough to cause either of us any lasting damage.

Monkton stirred beneath me, groaning.

"Get away," he told me. "Save yourself."

"I won't leave you here!"

"It's you they're after." He grimaced in evident pain. "They don't care about me."

I hauled him into a sitting position. "They don't care about anyone! That's the problem!"

He reached for my arm. The grip was feeble. "Where are they?"

But I didn't know the answer to that. I'd lost sight of them when the gargoyle had started to plummet.

"Can you get up?" I asked him. "Can you walk?"

He tried, bless him, but whatever hex Larch had cast had left him with little strength. It would be temporary; that was the only positive. The feeling was already coming back into his hands.

"Never mind," I told him, when our clumsy efforts to get him to his feet had failed. "We'll take shelter in the corner. I'll drag you over if I have to."

"My phone," he said, tapping weakly at his jacket pocket. Only ten minutes earlier he'd been a sharp-dressed man; now, so covered in dust and plaster was he, he resembled an alabaster copy of himself. A moving statue.

I suppose we both did.

Reaching into his pocket, I located his mobile and offered it to him. His fingers struggled to operate the screen, so I did it for him, found the number for the MOWPD switchboard, rang it and held it against his head so that he could both see and hear.

As he spoke to someone and gave our position, I surveyed the top of the monastery wall. Who had come to our rescue? And where had he gone?

"They're on their way," Monkton said, and I ended the call for him. "They won't be long."

"How do you know you can trust them?"

"They're our colleagues, Elise—"

I pointed at Larch. "He was your colleague." Such a likeable fellow. He'd had me fooled. "But he was in league with the Tweedles."

Monkton stretched his hands out, flexing and scrunching, more movement returning. "Just one bad egg, surely?"

I regarded Monkton, a colleague I'd known for years, cautiously. He was a good friend out of the office, too. How could I be sure the Labyrinthians hadn't managed to get to him? How far into the MOWPD had the organisation infiltrated?

I heard shouts echoing down the Paternoster Row tunnel. I needed to get to Wonderland; I had to make sure Wizard Dodo had received the book.

Abruptly, I stood and stepped away from Monkton.

He stared up at me, perhaps trying to read the change in my expression. "Elise?"

I wanted to believe he wasn't involved, that he was the same old Monkton Wyld he'd always been, but the way he'd been dragging his heels on the Dodo case— was he hiding something? Trying to protect someone?

Why hadn't the Tweedles killed him outright?

"You'll be okay now," I said. The voices were getting louder. I could hear the sound of heavy boots rushing through the tunnel. "I'll catch up with you in a bit."

"Elise?"

Without looking back, I took off down Silversmith Street. Larch had said there was a shortcut back to Cross Lane and onto Tudor Lane, but that had probably been a lie. I'd have to take a dog-leg and find my own way.

"Elise!" Monkton yelled, but ignoring him, I sped up.

$\approx$

As Monkton and the courtyard faded into the distance behind me, I pushed on. Without my phone—I should have taken it back from the now-deceased Larch—and my wand—buried under a ton of rubble somewhere—I couldn't contact the office to find out whether Snitch had made it.

I could only hope he had, and that he—and his robes and boots—hadn't been obliterated into a thin mist of nothingness.

I wouldn't think about that for now.

I pressed on.

Silversmith Street was a long thoroughfare. At the end closest to the monastery, it had a few shops—a bakery, a greengrocer, that kind of thing—and after that, lots of small, higgledy-piggledy houses. Halfway along, I began to see workshops. Signs with names like *Wizard Shinee's Silverware, The Sparkle Sisters' Treasure Chest, Dare to Dazzle* and *Cool Jewels* were hung outside, swinging on brackets above small windows, framing neat displays of jewellery, tankards, picture frames and such like.

An old street, aptly named.

Nowhere was open. Like most of Tumble Town's shops and businesses, they would conduct trading from ten or eleven in the morning until the wee hours, before closing and enjoying some downtime.

I slowed to a trot, looking for a left turn that would take me back in the direction of Cross Lane, but everywhere I tried appeared to empty out into yet another small courtyard, surrounded by more workshops.

Finally, at the moment of peak frustration, I located

a route. Bordered on both sides by quiet, decrepit dwellings, I jogged along, skipping over piles of rubbish and abandoned belongings, intent on getting back to what I was rapidly coming to think of as the more civilised part of Tumble Town.

At this time of the morning, getting on for eight, there were few people about. I hadn't passed anyone since leaving Monkton, but now, as I scurried along, I spotted a lone figure up ahead, his back to me, seemingly walking in the same direction I was taking.

I slowed again, carefully appraising the situation. I didn't want to rush headlong into an encounter I had no control over, but this person was walking *away* from me. He was tall, well dressed, wearing a top hat and carrying a stick. A cane or an umbrella perhaps. And he was alone.

I'd be fine.

Regulating my breathing, I walked steadily on. The man in front of me didn't appear to be making any great progress even though he, too, was walking. His speed was little more than a dawdle. I would have to pass him.

I was a few yards behind him when he halted.

I stopped, too.

He turned, slowly, and as he did so I realised I'd seen him before. The neatly trimmed beard. The black eyes.

Not someone I wanted to have a run-in with.

But at least he was alone.

I backed off and pivoted, intending to run back the way I'd come and find another route out of Silversmith Street. It wasn't to be. The bearded man's identical twin blocked my path.

"Great," I muttered.

I looked first from one, then to the other, and reluctantly backed up against the nearest wall. I needed something solid behind me. Two against one. It wouldn't be easy, but I knew how to handle myself in a fair fight. *If* these two were capable of a fair fight.

It was a big if.

They advanced steadily towards me, one from my left, the other from my right. I loosened my muscles, ready to let fly with a bit of witchy ninja, the self-defence skills I'd learned at the police academy. But then I realised both men were raising their walking canes.

But not to beat me to death with. No. I might have been able to fight them off if that had been the case.

Instead, as I looked on, I heard a slick whistling sound. *Sssssupp! Sssssupp!* And light caught the long, sharp, thin blades, at least twelve inches of lethal rod, that had shot out of the tips of the canes. Now I understood how Lily Budd had met her end.

I pressed further into the wall. I could try and take one man on, perhaps, but the end result would be the same. No matter which way I moved, either of these blades could slice me up like a side of cooked beef or run me through from belly to tail.

I was a dead woman.

My final option was to negotiate.

"Hey, guys?" I lifted my hands in surrender. "Let's talk about this."

No response. Each was as dead-eyed as the other.

The exact same expression as the Tweedles. I couldn't tell which of these men would be better to appeal to.

"I can get you the notebook," I tried. "I know where it is."

They were so close now, I could smell their cologne. Identical fragrances. I cringed, hunching my shoulders, screwing up my eyes, willing the earth to open up and swallow me. If it didn't, I'd be dead … in three and two and—

Ferocious barking to my left. Getting louder as it came closer. I dared to open my eyes in time to witness a pack of Tumble Town's feral dogs thundering down the lane towards us. Eyes on fire, snouts wrinkled, slobber flying, the ferocity of their anger evident in the growling emanating from deep within their chests.

My would-be assailants halted and, in one movement, turned to watch the dogs. Neither of their expressions changed, but their actual physicality did. For a few moments, I recognised the doughy faces of the Tweedles there, and then the pinched countenances of the hooked nose silver-haired old ladies … and the market inspector and his twin brother and—

The shapes shifted once more when the dogs were merely feet away.

No!

How was it possible?

The crows with the silver streaks!

Part bird, part man, both shapes took a huge leap. They lifted from the earth with ease, arms becoming wings that beat at the air. The dogs, almost rabid with anger, surged forward, jumping and snapping, but the men had taken flight. Growing smaller, taking more of the bird shape, shrinking, they soared away, disappearing behind the rooftops, leaving me alone with a ravenous pack of incensed canines.

A low whistle, long and imperative, and, as one, the dogs hushed. One or two of them whined, their ears flat against their heads. They turned, tails wagging and tongues lolling, to greet a lone figure walking towards us.

He reached down to pet the leaders before looking up at me and offering a slightly bashful smile.

"Well, hel-loo, darling," he said. "Fancy meeting you here."

The Viking.

CHAPTER 21

I let out a breath. Part relief, part exasperation, it was noticeably loud in the sudden silence. Thoroughly exhausted, I wasn't sure who was who anymore, or what side anyone was on. The world was topsy-turvy, or I was Elise through the looking glass … or … or … something.

"I should explain," he said, straightening up.

"Yes," I agreed. "You totally should." I pointed up the way he had come. "But we need to make haste. Will this path take me back to Tudor Lane?"

"Kind of." He nodded. "I'll show you."

He reached to help me—perhaps I looked as shaky as I felt—but I shrugged him away and he dropped his hand. Instead, we walked side by side, where the narrow lane allowed us to, the dogs straggling along behind us, stopping to sniff here and there, or examine a pile of rubbish, or cock a leg.

"What's your name?" I asked.

"I'm known in Tumble Town—and among the Labyrinthians—as Thomas Leominster."

Lemsta, Snitch had called him. "But that's not your real name?"

"No. My real name is … of no consequence."

I flicked a sideways look at him, lowering my voice. "You're Special Branch?"

He didn't say anything, just gave a single shallow nod.

"Were you involved with Lily—sorry—Annie?"

His chin drooped. "In real time. Before."

"Before?" I prompted.

"I've been working this patch for years. I took an apprenticeship as a tattoo artist and learned my trade so I could build up a decent cover. The more the underground came to know me, the more I was accepted. Eventually I infiltrated the Labyrinthians. But I knew Annie from when we did our training together. We shouldn't have become involved, but we did. When she was drafted into Tumble Town to gather information on the Tweedles, she chose to centre her investigation on the market inspector in Peachstone Market. We'd received prior intelligence about him."

"I see," I said. We'd come to a junction, where we turned left and then a quick right, the dogs ambling along in our wake.

"I was against her doing so, but she insisted it would all be fine. We weren't supposed to meet up, but we would. She would wait in the attic room of Old Mother Mae's florist. It had been deserted for so long we didn't imagine anyone would care. She could look out of the window upstairs and watch to see whether anyone was following me."

"I thought she was keeping tabs on you," I told him. "I was convinced you worked for them."

"That's what you were supposed to think, otherwise I would've been doing my job pretty badly." He offered me a wry smile.

With some relief, I realised we'd reached Cross Lane. I relaxed, just a little. "I'm so sorry about Annie. By all accounts she was a lovely woman."

"Thank you. She was. A little reckless at times, but that's the nature of the job. You can't do what we do unless you're prepared to take risks."

Hadn't he taken a huge one to save me? Sacrificed years of work? "What will happen to you now?"

"Ha." He smiled. "That's not up to me."

"You'll be pulled off the Labyrinthian case, though?"

"Oh yes. My cover is well and truly blown." I detected bitterness in his tone but didn't feel it was aimed at me. Nonetheless, I felt the need to apologise again.

"I'm sorry. My case overlapped with your operation, and you must think I was poking my nose in—"

"Don't worry about it," he said. "I'll be missed, but others are working on it."

Others?

He wouldn't be drawn any further, and we strolled the rest of the way to The Hat and Dashery in silence.

I pushed open the bottom door, expecting him to take his leave, but he followed me up the stairs.

"By crikey, Elise!" Hattie rushed to the door of the office to greet me. "We've been so worried!"

I strained to see around her, and to my absolute delight—and those are not the words I ever expected to use in conjunction with this individual—I saw Snitch, face pale and foot raised, sprawled on the comfy seats.

"Mr Lemsta!" Snitch widened his eyes and brushed crumbs from the front of his robes. I realised he was eating my stale prawn crackers.

Minsk was squatting on my desk. She stared at Thomas Leominster with her soft chocolate eyes and cocked her head in enquiry.

"All will become clear," I told her.

Wootton spoke into his phone. "Yeah, yeah, she's back," he was saying.

Meanwhile, Ezra was floating around in agitation—although he would never have admitted it—and Wizard Dodo was glowering at everyone, fed up with the noise and activity causing so much disruption this early in the day.

"I'm alright," I told them as Hattie reached out to embrace me. I accepted the hug, showering her with a couple of ounces of plaster dust and statue debris in an effort to make her feel included in our adventures. "Any news on Monkton?" I asked.

Wootton replaced the receiver into its cradle. "That was him. He wanted to know if you'd made it back alright."

Concern? Or was he sending the boys over to sort me out once and for all?

We needed to be quick.

"Snitch?" I extracted myself from Hattie's tight grasp. "Did you manage to do as I asked?"

"All of it, DC Liddell."

Thank goodness. "You're a superstar. Remind me to give you a pay rise."

"You don't pay me." Snitch looked taken aback.

"Well, I do now."

"Awesome!" That brought a little colour into his cheeks.

"Now, the book?" I asked.

"I've got it," Ezra said, and it floated from his desk, through the air and into my hand.

As I caught it, there was no mistaking the shimmer of energy. "Excellent." I placed it gently in front of Wizard Dodo.

He glared at me. "What's this?"

"That's what I would like you to find out," I said. "Please."

"Why should I?"

"Because you want to know who was behind your murder, and I do too. I think this book may help us."

He waved his hand over it. As he did so, the buzz of energy was unmistakable. Wootton moved his chair, scraping it along the floor, to get a better view. Hattie and Thomas drew closer. Minsk hopped across the chasms between desks, situating herself by my right hand, her whiskers twitching. Even Snitch moved from his comfortable spot.

Dodo glanced around. Despite the defiance of his tone, the light in his eyes had changed. "What makes you think I can find out?"

"I know you can," I told him. "Because that's what you do."

Without another word, he smoothed the surface of the book, his hands not physically touching it, but even so, the cover undulated under his touch. He wiggled his fingers, and the pages began to turn, slowly, creating a slight breeze that blew the dust from my jacket and hair as I leaned over the desk and watched.

"*Omaloiahtowishtrasavarudavashmedak*," he intoned, his hands crossing over in the air, then out, then back again. "*Medawawashnakiviov. Omaloiahtowishtrasavarudavashmedak!*"

He repeated the chants and the movements several times. The pages, at first blank, shivered. Then faint watery marks of long faded ink began to appear. Slight scratches. Blobs. Lines.

"*Omaloiahtowishtrasavarudavashmedak. Reveal yourself!*" the wizard ordered, his voice authoritative and yet strangely quiet, as though there were spirits in the room he didn't want to disturb.

The notebook vibrated, the energy it emitted causing the air around us to hum, until at last, the writing was visible, the pages full of scrawl. I thought I recognised the flourishes and the twirls. Had this once belonged to the market inspector? Was that where Annie had found it?

Wizard Dodo quietened and gently pushed the book towards me. I picked it up. The writing was legible. Flicking through it, the gravity of the contents slowly dawned on me. I gasped and showed it to Minsk and Tom. "The Labyrinthians! This is a record of activities.

There are lists in here of hideouts and personnel. Their contacts. Suppliers. Enough to bring the whole organisation to its knees!"

"That's incredible!" Minsk clapped her soft paws together. "I want a copy. I'll get the Dark Squad on it straight away!"

"Is there anyone we know on the list?" Ezra asked. "Is there an easy way of finding out?"

"There are masses of names there," Wootton said. "Please don't tell me you want me to type it all out."

"Now there's an idea," I said. "But in the interests of expediency, perhaps you could scan it and send a copy to Minsk and one to"—I gestured at Thomas—"Special Branch?"

I flicked through the book some more. "It's actually set out quite well. Perhaps not as many names as we thought. Some are duplicated. Put into lists." I stopped and took a moment. "MOWPD," I said, then flicked backwards, then forwards, then back to the MOWPD page. "This is a list of officers, both serving and retired, who are or have been involved with the Labyrinthians." I scanned the list. Suddenly I could hardly breathe.

"This is gold dust," Minsk enthused.

"What?" Ezra caught my stillness. "Someone you know?"

"Taurus," I said.

"Taurus?" Thomas repeated.

"That was the name!" Wootton jolted backwards. "I heard them talking about him when I was a captive in the cellar. I thought they said Thor, but no, it was Taurus."

"The head of the Bulls," I added. "The Labyrinthians' henchmen. The thugs on the street. Their leader—"

"What about him?" Minsk pawed at my thigh in impatience. I was holding the book too high for her to read.

The relief made my knees weak. Not Monkton, thank goodness.

"Not a him. A her. Superintendent Yvonne Ibeus. Chief Inspector. She's been pulling the strings all along. Putting pressure on DCI Wyld to drop the case. Telling him the Dodo murder was solved. Making poor Monkton's life a total misery."

Ezra cleared his throat. There was a small noise behind us. I turned to see Monkton leaning against the door jamb. His colour was better, but he still looked as though he had been buried beneath a rockfall.

"You'd better fill me in," he said. "It sounds like some of my superiors have a few questions to answer."

EPILOGUE

By the time Monkton and a team of his top, most trusted—and newly re-vetted—officers went in search of Superintendent Ibeus, she'd disappeared. But at least now we knew who had wanted Wizard Dodo dead.

The Labyrinthians were quick to go to ground, too. Despite all the names and hideouts, and even though the MOWPD worked in conjunction with both the Dark Squad and Special Branch, by the time their teams raided the addresses in the notebook, everywhere had been abandoned. In some cases, where there might have been incriminating evidence in the form of computers, phones or other records, mysterious fires had broken out overnight. Tumble Town had stunk of smoke and burnt plastic for days.

We convened a catch-up meeting in The Pig and Pepper a few days later. Charles Lynch, the pub's proprietor, propped up the bar and scowled at us while his latest bar person toiled to manage all the drink orders. I could tell Charles wasn't happy about the sheer number of police officers who'd popped by. We were frightening all his regular—and highly dubious—clients away.

I sipped at a sparkling mineral water and sighed.

Not for the first time.

"What's up, Grandma?" Wootton asked.

"I feel like we failed," I said. "And I hate to fail."

"But we didn't fail," Minsk argued. "Far from it."

"We haven't made a single arrest!" I moaned. That didn't count as a success in my book.

"We effectively shut them down," Ezra pointed out. "They're not going to peer above the parapet anytime soon."

"Let's hope not!" Hattie was in her element. Dressed in a top hat of peacock blue, with a plume of feathers spouting from the side, she was never happier than when she had her friends around her—especially Minsk. Even Dodo had agreed to join us. Still cantankerous, but slightly more mellow now that we'd put a face and a name to the person who had given the order to have him disposed of.

"No wonder poor Cerys and Kevin Makepeace had no choice but to follow her wishes," I lamented. "Such a shame they couldn't have spoken to you."

Monkton, nursing a pint of Hoodwinker, nodded. "And yet, what could I have done? I'd have gone to Grisham Farley, but chances are he wouldn't have believed me."

"It's a tragedy all round," Minsk agreed.

"What bothers me—" Snitch's quiet voice drifted out

of the corner, where he was hiding in the shadows, only the white cast on his foot bright enough to see in the muted lights of the pub. "What really bothers me, is that nobody knows what happened to Wizard Dodo's books."

I nodded. "Cerys told me they were taken in as evidence. At the time, I didn't have any reason to disbelieve that."

"I told you they weren't," Monkton pointed out.

"I should have followed that up."

"I'd like them back," Dodo agreed. He shook his finger at me. "You'd better make that your next case, girlie."

Misogynistic old trout. "Oi! That's DI to you."

"DI?" Snitch gasped. "Did you get a promotion?"

Wootton and Ezra dissolved into giggles. Hattie laughed along with them, although I think she was just tipsy on white wine spritzers, to be honest.

Even Minsk, with her tumbler full of Blue Goblin, snickered. "So, what *is* next for the Wonderland Detective Agency?" she asked.

"That's a good question," I answered. "Obviously I'm going to keep my ear to the ground where the Labyrinthians are concerned."

"As will I." Minsk nodded. "And seeing as I'm shorter than you, I'll be much better at it."

I grinned. "We do have a number of cases on the books—"

"Widow Lefferty." Wootton had recovered himself sufficiently that he could rejoin the conversation. "That's a tricky one."

"It really is," I agreed. "Interesting, though. I probably need to focus on that first, but you know me ..." I shrugged happily. "If something else came along, I'd jump in with both feet!"

"Let's hope you don't break one of them," Snitch sniffed.

Minsk raised her glass. "I'm sure it won't be long till you find yourself up to your neck in another murder!"

She wasn't wrong.

COMING SOON

The Curious Incident at The Pig and Pepper: Wonderland Detective Agency Book 4

These pilgrims are pious ... and they're taking no prisoners!

Since giving up the booze—bar a small hiccup here and there—ex-Ministry of Witches detective, Elise Liddell hasn't had much call to hang out in bars. So imagine her surprise when the generally antagonistic landlord of The Pig and Pepper calls on her for assistance.

It seems Charles Lynch's regulars are being scared away by mysterious spectres. It's hitting him where it hurts. Right in the pocket.

Elise agrees to help. After all, the pub is her local, and she isn't generally spooked by the paranormal.

However, the apparitions turn out to be monks.

Malevolent monks!

Elise will need to rely on her friends, her wiles and

all her resources, if she's going to unravel this curiosity of a mystery!

Join Elise and her zany sidekicks—Minsk the white rabbit, the ghosts of Wizard Dodo and her partner DC Ezra Izax, Wootton the office manager, Hattie Dashery, Rich the Snitch, and ex-boss Monkton Wyld—in the fourth thrilling instalment of the **Wonderland Detective Agency**.

Order The Curious Incident at The Pig and Pepper on Amazon

Or sign up to Jeannie Wycherley's newsletter for updates

PLEASE LEAVE A REVIEW

Have you enjoyed *Tweedledumb and Tweedledie*?
Please leave me a review on Amazon or Goodreads.
Reviews help spread the word about my work, which is
great for me because I find new readers!
And why not join my mailing list to find out more
about what I'm up to and what is coming out next? Just
pop along to my website and fill in the quick form.
You'll find me at jeanniewycherley.co.uk
If you'd like to join my closed author group, you'll find
it here at
https://www.facebook.com/
groups/JeannieWycherleysFiends/
Please let me know you've reviewed one of my books
when you apply.

***The Creature from the Grim Mire: A Humorous Sci-fi,
Time Travel and Alien Cozy Contact Mystery***
**There's no chance of a quiet life when you've aliens
in your attic!**
Felicity Westmacott craves solitude.
But something with a hearty appetite is stalking the
moor and terrifying the locals.
And things going bump in the night puts paid to her
equilibrium.
As does the mysterious appearance of an elderly
gentleman who claims to be a time traveller. Obviously
as nutty as a fruitcake, he wants her to run a creche.
For baby aliens.
Now her secret's out and other people are interested in
Felicity's unusual house guests.
Her 'children' are in terrible danger.
Will Felicity save her young charges? Or will she opt to
finish her novel instead?
Find out *in The Creature from the Grim Mire.*

If you've ever wondered what HG Wells got up to in his spare time, you'll love this alien invasion tale set on Dartmoor in South Devon, UK. This is the perfect light-hearted read for lovers of humorous sci-fi mysteries or cozy animal mysteries, or indeed anyone seeking a bit of fun escapism with a cup of tea and a slice of cake. But keep an eye on your snacks – there are hungry aliens loose. Some of them can eat their body weight in Custard Creams!

The Creature from the Grim Mire is a collaboration between father and daughter, Peter Alderson Sharp (*The Dragan Kelly Books*) and Jeannie Wycherley (the *Wonky Inn* books, *Crone, The Municipality of Lost Souls* etc.).

ALSO BY JEANNIE WYCHERLEY

The Complete Wonky Inn Series (in chronological reading order)
The Wonkiest Witch: Wonky Inn Book 1
The Ghosts of Wonky Inn: Wonky Inn Book 2
Weird Wedding at Wonky Inn: Wonky Inn Book 3
The Witch Who Killed Christmas: Wonky Inn
Christmas Special
Fearful Fortunes and Terrible Tarot: Wonky Inn Book 4
The Mystery of the Marsh Malaise: Wonky Inn Book 5
The Mysterious Mr Wylie: Wonky Inn Book 6
The Great Witchy Cake Off: Wonky Inn Book 7
Vengeful Vampire at Wonky Inn: Wonky Inn Book 8
Witching in a Winter Wonkyland: A Wonky Inn
Christmas Cozy Special
A Gaggle of Ghastly Grandmamas: Wonky Inn Book 9
Magic, Murder and a Movie Star: Wonky Inn Book 10
O' Witchy Town of Whittlecombe: A Wonky Inn
Christmas Cozy Special

Judge, Jury and Jailhouse Rockcakes: Wonky Inn
Book 11
A Midsummer Night's Wonky: Wonky Inn Book 12
Halloween Heebie-Geebies: Wonky Inn Book 13
(Release Date September 2021)
Owl I want for Witchmas is Hoo: A Wonky Inn
Christmas Cozy Mystery (Release Date October 2021)
Oh Mummy: Wonky Inn Book 14 (Release Date March
2022)

Spellbound Hound
Ain't Nothing but a Pound Dog: Spellbound Hound
Magic and Mystery Book 1
A Curse, a Coven and a Canine: Spellbound Hound
Magic and Mystery Book 2
Bark Side of the Moon: Spellbound Hound Magic and
Mystery Book 3
Master of Puppies: Spellbound Hound Magic and
Mystery Book 4 (2022 TBC)

The Municipality of Lost Souls (2020)
Midnight Garden: The Extra Ordinary World Novella
Series Book 1 (2019)
Beyond the Veil (2018) http://mybook.to/BTV
Crone (2017) http://mybook.to/CroneJW
A Concerto for the Dead and Dying (short story, 2018)
http://mybook.to/ConcertoDead
Deadly Encounters: A collection of short stories (2017)
http://mybook.to/DeadlyEncounters

Keepers of the Flame: A love story (Novella, 2018)
http://mybook.to/keepers

Non-Fiction

Losing my best Friend: Thoughtful support for those
affected by dog bereavement or pet loss (2017) http://
mybook.to/LosingMyBestFriend

Follow Jeannie Wycherley

Find out more at on the website https://www.
jeanniewycherley.co.uk/
You can tweet Jeannie https://
twitter.com/Thecushionlady
Or visit her on Facebook for her fiction https://www.
facebook.com/jeanniewycherley/
Follow Jeannie on Instagram (for bears and books)
https://www.instagram.com/jeanniewycherley/
Sign up for Jeannie's newsletter on her website https://
www.subscribepage.com/JeannieWycherleyWonky

Printed in Great Britain
by Amazon